"No." April twisted her fingers together. "You don't understand."

"You're right. I don't. And, honey, at this moment I don't really want to." There was a lot of lust in the look he settled on her.

"And I don't really want to tell you. But, like I said before, you set a high bar for full disclosure. So whether you want to or not, you have to hear this."

"Okay, then. If I agree to listen, can we pick up where we just left off?"

"Trust me. You're not going to want to do that." When Will found out she was a scheming, underhanded, devious witch, he wouldn't want anything to do with her.

"Let me be the judge of that. Because right now I want to kiss you more than anything. And unless you tell me you're a man, which I know for a fact isn't true, there's not much you could say to change my mind." His blue eyes turned darker and focused a lot of intensity on her mouth.

* * *

THE BACHELORS OF BLACKWATER LAKE:
They won't be single for long!

Dear Reader,

Do you ever think about the one who got away? That person who made your toes curl and your heart beat faster the first time you saw them? But for some reason things didn't work out. Only later, when your heart healed a little, did you think about what had happened to them since the split and wonder if you could have done something different.

In *How to Land Her Lawman*, April Kennedy gets a chance to find out. Will Fletcher left her behind in Blackwater Lake and moved to Chicago to become a police detective. She was supposed to follow but life got in the way, and their relationship fell apart. Now he's back in town as the acting sheriff for his recuperating father. April's best friend, who also happens to be Will's sister, comes up with a brilliant (if she does say so herself) plan to deal with him. It starts out as payback but turns into something else. And in this story, revenge is a dish served very hot!

I feel incredibly lucky to be able to make a living at doing what I love. Life so often doesn't happen the way we hope, but in a romance novel you can always count on everything working out in a good way. I sincerely hope you enjoy April and Will's do-over on the journey to finding their happily-ever-after.

Happy reading!

Teresa Southwick

How to Land Her Lawman

Teresa Southwick

HARLEQUIN® SPECIAL EDITION®

Recycling programs
for this product may
not exist in your area.

ISBN-13: 978-0-373-65951-7

How to Land Her Lawman

Copyright © 2016 by Teresa Southwick

Printed in U.S.A.

Teresa Southwick lives with her husband in Las Vegas, the city that reinvents itself every day. An avid fan of romance novels, she is delighted to be living out her dream of writing for Harlequin.

Books by Teresa Southwick

Harlequin Special Edition

The Bachelors of Blackwater Lake

The Widow's Bachelor Bargain
A Decent Proposal
The Rancher Who Took Her In
One Night with the Boss
Finding Family...and Forever?

Montana Mavericks:
What Happened at the Wedding?

An Officer and a Maverick

Montana Mavericks: 20 Years in the Saddle!

From Maverick to Daddy

Mercy Medical Montana

Her McKnight in Shining Armor
The Doctor's Dating Bargain

Montana Mavericks: Back in the Saddle

The Maverick's Christmas Homecoming

Montana Mavericks: The Texans are Coming!

Her Montana Christmas Groom

Men of Mercy Medical

The Doctor and the Single Mom
Holding Out for Doctor Perfect
To Have the Doctor's Baby
Cindy's Doctor Charming

Visit the Author Profile page
at Harlequin.com for more titles.

To Kate Carlisle, Christine Rimmer
and Susan Mallery, the best plot group ever.
You make it so much fun to play "what if?"

Chapter One

William Fletcher would rather face an armed felon than
have the conversation he was about to have with his ex-
girlfriend. But, as the saying went, this town wasn't big
enough for the both of them. For better or worse, this summer he was the acting sheriff in Blackwater Lake and she
was a freelance photographer who occasionally did work
for the department. She also had a studio on Main Street
across from his office.

There was no way he wouldn't see her and the sooner
this confrontation was behind him the better.

He'd been watching the Photography Shop all morning,
waiting for her to be alone, and now stood on the sidewalk
in front of the sheriff's office ready to head over. Hesitation was costing him a hell of a lot of time when there
was work to do. He looked left, then right before crossing
the street. Her window had big, fancy letters telling the
establishment's name, then smaller print in the right hand

corner proclaiming April Kennedy, Photographer. There was a list of services in the right corner—Portraits, Family Sittings, Weddings and Special Occasions.

Will stared at the displayed dance-hall girl and gambler forms with cutouts where the tourists put their faces for a fun souvenir picture of a visit to Blackwater Lake, Montana. Technically he was a visitor but definitely not a tourist. Born and raised in this town, he was only here to help out and would go back to being a detective for Chicago PD in three months when his dad, the real sheriff, got a clean bill of health to resume his job.

"Man up, Fletcher," he muttered. "What's the worst that could happen?"

She could cry. The thought made him cringe.

He'd seen her do that and it ripped him up. But that was a lot of years ago. He didn't know whether or not she'd still be angry but the first face-to-face since then was no doubt going to be awkward.

Will braced himself and pushed open the glass door. The bell above it rang as he walked inside. There was no one in the front but a familiar female voice called out, "I'll be right with you."

It was cheerful and sweet and the sound echoed inside him, stirring the cobwebs of tucked-away memories. It was impossible not to notice the framed photos displayed on the walls, examples of her skill as a photographer. There were individuals, families, babies. Some were black-and-white portraits, dramatic and really good. There'd always been something about April that people responded to, something that made them relax and allowed the camera to capture a special look or smile. The only black-and-whites he usually saw were cop cars, so this was a pleasant change.

"I'm so sorry I kept you waiting—" April Kennedy

came through the open doorway and froze in her tracks when she saw him.

"Hi," he said.

At one time they'd practically been engaged, but Will felt as if he was seeing her for the first time. Her shiny long brown hair was pulled into a ponytail with wisps coming loose around her face. She was wearing jeans and a purple Photography Shop T-shirt that clung to every sweet curve. Big hazel eyes stared back at him and right now they were more green than brown, which meant she wasn't happy to see him. He couldn't blame her.

"Will."

"You look really good, April."

"Thanks. So do you."

"I'm pretty sure you didn't want to tell me that, so I'll take it as a compliment."

"Gotta be honest." She shrugged.

"And I've always liked that about you."

"I heard you were coming back to Blackwater Lake."

He didn't have to ask how she'd heard. April was best friends with his younger sister, Kim. She and her teenage son lived with their dad and Will had moved into his old room for the summer. One big happy family again. The backyard of April's little house was separated by an alley from his dad's rear yard. Hank Fletcher had watched over April and her single mom because it was the neighborly thing to do. And, unlike himself, his dad had been there when April's mom died of breast cancer. The Fletchers had kind of unofficially adopted her, so of course they would warn her that he was coming back.

"The thing is, this is a small town," he started.

"As opposed to Chicago." Her voice was as icy as a Windy City blizzard.

"Right. There's no way we won't run into each other

and I wanted to make sure the first time wasn't public and uncomfortable for you."

He'd checked one out of two boxes. This wasn't public but she had to be as uncomfortable as he was.

"Kim told you to do this." She wasn't asking a question.

"My sister mentioned that it would be better if the first time we saw each other it was just the two of us, without a big crowd of people looking on. And talking about it." Because the only thing folks in Blackwater Lake were better at than being neighborly was gossiping.

"Still, you didn't have to take her advice. It's actually very thoughtful of you, Will." Her tone implied his consideration was unexpected.

Or maybe it just sounded that way because his conscience was passing the words through the guilt filter. Either way, he figured it was a good idea to clear the air. "I don't think I ever apologized for what happened in Chicago."

"You mean the time I came to surprise you and a woman answered the door wearing nothing but your shirt?"

"Yeah. That." He was staring at her mouth, the way she pressed her lips together. It had always made him want to kiss her and unfortunately now was no exception. Normally it was comforting knowing things didn't change but this wasn't one of those times.

"You tried to apologize, actually." She met his gaze directly. "But I wasn't speaking to you, so that made it kind of hard."

"Well, let me say it now. I'm sorry for what happened."

"Let it go, Will. I have. That was a long time ago. It was my idea not to be exclusive when you went to Chicago and entered the police academy. It seemed the right thing to do since I couldn't go with you and everyone knows long-distance relationships are a challenge. We found out the hard way how true that is. Technically we didn't have a relationship and it still fell apart."

Will remembered trying to talk her into going to Chicago with him, but her mom had just been diagnosed. April had never known her dad and wouldn't abandon the mother who had raised her daughter alone and always put her first. She'd suggested they date other people but keep in touch and after a year reevaluate things between them. He was glad she hadn't forgotten that.

"I didn't expect you not to date," she said. "And you did."

"For what it's worth, you were right about everything."

"Things happen for the best. Water under the bridge. Let bygones be bygones. And any other cliché you can think of to put this behind you." She shrugged as if it made no difference to her.

"Okay, then."

Will felt oddly dissatisfied with her response. Maybe the altitude was getting to him. That was the best explanation he could come up with for why he wasn't completely relieved that she didn't scream or cry or seem the least bit emotional about what had happened. Or maybe he was simply an egotistical jerk who expected her to still be a little bothered about something he'd done six years ago.

Possibly his reaction was colored by the fact that he'd married the woman wearing nothing but his shirt and it had been a failure. On top of that, he'd always had the nagging feeling that what he'd done to April was the biggest mistake he'd ever made. For a man who hated to fail, doing it twice at the same time didn't sit very well. And it was kind of annoying that she seemed completely at peace with how things had turned out.

"So, if that's all—" She cocked a thumb over her shoulder toward the back room, where a camera sat on a tripod.

"Just so you know, I'll be here until the end of summer while Dad is recuperating from his open-heart surgery."

"That was a scare." She put her hand to her chest. The first honest emotion she'd exhibited since he'd walked in. "First the heart attack, then surgery. It was like watching the Rock of Gibraltar crack. Your sister has been his diet-and-exercise drill sergeant ever since he got out of the hospital and started cardiac rehab."

"Kim is hard to say no to." He was here talking to April, wasn't he? "The sheriff has always protected the citizens of his town first and himself a distant second. Maybe he saw God when the doc put him under for the procedure because right after he got out of the hospital he asked me to fill in for him. Then he got the mayor and town council to approve my temporary appointment."

"It would be just like him to push himself to go back to work too soon. I'm sure your family is glad to have you here." Her tone said she felt differently. "And a good thing you could take extended leave from your job."

Maybe the job needed time off from him. Between that and his sister nagging him to not be an ass and do it for Dad, he had decided to take one for team Fletcher. All he was willing to say was, "I have a lot of days on the Chicago PD books."

"So you're the sheriff now." She folded her arms over her chest.

"Acting, but yeah. And I wanted to make sure I can count on you for freelance work when needed." Sometimes there were multicar accidents that required photos with more detail than an untrained photographer could capture with a cell phone. Insurance companies were funny that way when a settlement was involved. Mug shots were part of the official record.

"Of course I'll continue the arrangement. It's important that Hank knows everything will go smoothly in his absence. Just as if he was at the wheel."

"So you're doing it for Dad."

"Absolutely. After you and I didn't work out, you got what's-her-name, but I got your family. I'd do anything for them."

"They're lucky to have you."

"No." She shook her head and her ponytail swung from side to side. "I'm the lucky one."

The weird feeling in his chest felt a lot like envy. He was jealous of her loyalty to his dad, sister and nephew even though he'd given up any right to her commitment. He might not have cheated officially but it was a betrayal of spirit. And he still didn't feel as if the air was cleared.

"I should have told you I was dating someone, but I didn't want to hurt you."

"And that worked out so well." She smiled, but it didn't turn her hazel eyes from green to warm. They went almost chocolaty brown. "Golly, this has been fun, but I have someone coming in for a sitting and need to get things set up."

"Okay. I didn't mean to keep you."

"No problem. I appreciate you stopping by. Now when we run into each other it won't be awkward at all. See you around, Will." She turned and walked into the back.

"Bye, April."

He left her shop and felt like gum on someone's shoe. Kim had said seeing her would take the heat off, but she couldn't have been more wrong. The heat was on and it had nothing to do with their history and everything to do with the beautiful, sexy woman April Kennedy still was. And when had she gotten so confident and sassy? So independent?

That was different. She was the same—but different.

Man, it was going to be a long, hot summer.

* * *

April heard a knock on the sliding glass door in her kitchen and hurried to answer it. Kim Fletcher was standing on the back porch and she yanked the other woman inside.

"Thanks for coming. I'm glad you didn't have plans with Luke."

"I'd have canceled if I did. You said it was vital that we talk. What's up?"

Her friend was engaged to be married this summer to another teacher at Blackwater Lake High School, where she worked in the English Department. Luke was the football coach in addition to teaching science. Her son, Tim, played freshman football and approved of the man his mom was going to marry. She'd found her happily-ever-after and April was glad at least one of them had.

"Did anyone at home know you were coming over here?"

Kim gave her a "really?" look. "News flash. My father, brother and son are guys. They don't pay any attention to me. I could announce that I was going to be a fire eater in the circus and they'd say 'Have a good time.' I'm invisible to them."

"Okay." With Will in Chicago all this time, April had forgotten how inconvenient it was that her best friend and her ex were siblings. Who now temporarily lived together under the same roof. All she'd thought about was her own personal emergency and made an SOS call to her bestie. "I need to talk to you and the conversation calls for wine."

"Twist my arm." Kim held it out. "I promise I won't say no."

Kim Fletcher was pretty and for a long time April hadn't thought about how much she looked like her brother. Same blue eyes and brown hair, although her friend's was heavily highlighted, making her look more blonde. The thought of manly, masculine Will with highlighted hair almost made her smile.

After April poured Chardonnay into the two wine-glasses waiting on the kitchen island, they carried them to the family room and sat on the sofa.

Kim scooted back and tucked her legs up beside her. "You saw Will."

April sipped her wine then nodded. "I'd say you're psychic except that he admitted the meeting was your idea. To avoid an awkward, public encounter."

"You're welcome," Kim said.

"Hold it. I'm not on the gratitude train yet." April had been jittery and uneasy ever since seeing him again. She liked status quo and really wanted it restored but wasn't quite sure how to stuff all the emotional junk back in the jar. "It might have been better to take my chances. Maybe I wouldn't have run into him at all."

"Seriously?" The other woman gave her a you're-kidding-yourself look. "This town is the size of a postage stamp. The sheriff's office is right across the street from your shop. He's living not very far from your back door. If you really believe your paths won't cross in the three months he'll be here, you're in serious denial."

"I know. And you're right. But I wish you'd warned me."

Kim shook her head. "Surprise was better. Your reaction had to be natural. Unscripted."

April wanted to crawl into a hole when she thought about how it had gone seeing Will again. She hadn't been prepared and preparation was her thing. When she got in the car, she mentally plotted the route to her destination. Writing a grocery list started on aisle one and ended at produce. For a photography sitting she always had cameras, lenses, backdrops and props ready.

Even though he lived in Chicago, she knew Will would return to Blackwater Lake from time to time because his family was here. Kim had always warned her when he was visiting and she'd successfully avoided him. In fact she hadn't seen him at the hospital when his dad had surgery, but she knew he'd been there. She managed to stay out of his way. None of that stopped her from picturing how a meeting between them would go and in her imagination she'd always been less tongue-tied, her wit sharp as a stiletto. Her moment to make him sorry he hadn't waited for her.

"I don't know about unscripted," April said ruefully, "but it was unsomething."

"How was it? Seeing him again, I mean?" Sympathy gathered in Kim's eyes.

"He looks good." Really good. April hated to admit it, but he'd been right that she hadn't wanted to tell him so. "And it's nice of him to put his life on hold and come back to help the family."

Kim nodded absently. "Don't get me wrong. I love my brother. But I think there's something going on with him. Career-wise, I mean. There have been family crises—God knows I was one. Being an unwed teenage mother certainly qualifies for family-crisis material. Mom was killed in that car accident not long after he entered the police academy. It's not to say he doesn't care because I know he does. But he never put work on hold to be here for us before."

"Has he said anything?"

The other woman shook her head. "No. He just seems edgy, tense. Different. I don't know. Maybe I'm seeing ghosts where there aren't any."

"Maybe you should talk to him about it." April didn't have the right to be involved in his life and it annoyed her that she couldn't shut off her concern. "Get him to open up."

"You know better than anyone that my brother doesn't talk about stuff. Right now getting Dad back on his feet is the most important thing. Will stepping in for him as sheriff means Dad won't worry about this town and can focus on getting strong again."

"That's true." But April's life would be far less complicated if the sheriff trusted someone besides his son. No matter how well Chicago PD trained its officers. On top of that Will knew Blackwater Lake inside and out. There was no doubt he would take good care of the town. "I just wish I knew how to get through the next three months with Will here."

Thoughtfully, Kim tapped a fingernail against her wineglass. "A statement like that makes me think you're still in love with my brother."

"No. You're wrong. It's been a lot of years." April rejected that suggestion with every fiber of her being. "That would just be stupid. Fool me once shame on you. Fool me twice, shame on me."

"Hmm." The woman stared at her. "Where there's smoke, there's fire."

"A cliché? From Blackwater Lake High School's favorite honors English teacher?"

"Clichés work because they convey a lot of truth. In this case, you seem to have strong feelings about seeing Will again. That doesn't happen if you don't care." She finished the wine in her glass. "Hence, smoke and fire."

"I can assure you that what I feel for Will isn't love. It's ancient history. I've had relationships since him."

"But you make sure they never work. You always find an excuse to not take things to the next level. As soon as a guy even hints at getting serious, you shut down and blow him off completely."

April shrugged. "So sue me. I want something special, to be swept away. Settling for less isn't an option for me. And you have to kiss a lot of frogs…"

"Maybe." Kim didn't sound convinced. "Or maybe you need closure with the first frog. Maybe you never moved on after Will hopped away."

"Finding him with another woman seemed like closure to me." But, darn it, today he'd looked genuinely sorry about what had happened.

"Then why did you call me over here to talk? What's the problem?" Her friend didn't sound annoyed as much as frustrated that she couldn't help.

"I guess the problem is that I really want to hate him. That would make this summer so much easier and less awkward. Hate is simple, straightforward and sensible. I can deal with hate. But he was *nice*."

"Rest assured I'll give him a stern talking-to about that." There was a teasing look in Kim's eyes.

"You know what I mean," April protested.

"I do. And I still say your problem is about closure."

"I wish I could be the opposite of a bear and hibernate in the summer. Go to sleep and wake up after Labor Day. If I haven't gotten closure by now, I'm never going to."

"Maybe there's a way." Her friend had a familiar expression on her face, the one that hinted inspiration was knocking on the door.

"Enlighten me." April's interest was piqued.

"Seduce him."

"What? Are you crazy?"

"In the best possible way, or so my fiancé says. That Luke is a keeper," she said with a sigh.

"No argument. But can we go back to where you just told me to seduce your brother in order to find closure?"

"And then dump him. Did I leave that part out?"

"Yes." April sat up straighter. "How does that give me closure?"

"Your last breakup was situational and one-sided. Your emotions are stuck in neutral. Flirt with him. Have a fling. When he's putty in your hands tell him Jean Luc, your winter-ski-instructor-lover, is due to arrive any day and you have to end your summer dalliance."

"On top of the fact that there is no Jean Luc, I don't think I can do that."

"Don't you see?" Kim said, warming to her proposal. "You finally have your chance for revenge. Of course you can do it."

April shook her head. "I'm not that person."

"Look, I know you're really nice. It's why I love you and why we've been best friends forever. But, trust me on this, you need to get some perspective and the best way to do that is to take control."

"But he's your brother," April protested.

"All the better. I give you my permission. If I approve no one can judge you harshly."

"But I'm not very good at seduction."

"You'll be fine. And I have a feeling it won't take much effort or finesse. You need this and revenge is swift and satisfying. Humility would give Will a little character."

April was starting to weaken. "But he married Miss Naked-Under-His-Shirt. And now they're divorced." Surely she could be forgiven for feeling the tiniest bit of satisfaction about that. "I would think that gives him a lot of character credits."

"No. He left her, remember?" Kim made a face. "I never liked that woman."

April loved her for that. "Still, it seems inherently dishonest. Because it is inherently dishonest."

"If you flirt with him and he responds, how is that dishonest? It would be if you hated him, but you said you can't do that."

This whole scene tipped into weird territory because that actually made a twisted sort of sense. "So you really don't think this is a despicably underhanded thing to do? Intentionally flirting with every intention of dumping him? That's the very definition of premeditated."

"You're so overthinking this." Kim sighed. "Just get my brother in bed, then say goodbye. He's moving back to his life in Chicago at the end of the summer anyway. The two of you have a good time and it ends. Things will work out. Trust me."

Famous last words.

But a lot of what her friend said made sense. It was a proactive way to deal with the problem. If he felt nothing for her, no way would there be sex. That in itself would be confirmation they'd never have worked out. Pretty much all she had to do was be nice to him and see what happened.

She leaned over and hugged her friend. "That's why I needed to talk to you."

"Happy to help."

"You definitely did," April said.

And now she had a plan.

Chapter Two

April pulled the chicken casserole out of the oven and smiled at the cheerful bubbling around the edges of the perfectly browned noodles. The crispy parts were her favorite.

"Okay, then," she said to herself, "Operation Poke the Bear is officially under way."

And officially time to get in touch with her inner flirt. Hopefully she still had some of that mojo although that would presuppose she ever had any in the first place. Anything too obvious would be, well…too obvious. It would be a dead giveaway if she walked up to him and said, "Hey, Mr. Sexy Pants, come on up and see me sometime."

When she started to hyperventilate it was a signal that she needed to get a grip. Less than twenty-four hours ago Kim had floated this idea. A slow start didn't mean she'd lose the race and as long as she didn't do anything out of character, no warning flags would be raised.

"Okay. Here goes." She put a lid on the dish, then slid the whole thing into a casserole carrier and food warmer.

April grabbed the dish and went out her kitchen door, stepping onto the patio. She looked around at her neatly trimmed grass and the flowers in cheerful bloom. A sidewalk led to the alley and she smiled, remembering that her mother put it in because there was already a worn path in the grass from April going to Will's house. Or him coming here.

That seemed like a lifetime ago, but still a stab of sadness went through her. She still missed her mom and probably always would. Seeing Will again had stirred up a lot of memories, some good but a whole lot of them not.

Sighing, she walked across the alley, up the three steps to the Fletchers' back door and knocked loudly.

Moments later it opened and Will stood there. "April. Hi."

"Hey. I made a casserole for your dad. And everyone." Oh, God, her mind was going blank. "I've gotten in the habit of doing this since he got out of the hospital. It was a helpless feeling not being able to do anything for him, so I made food and brought it over. This is heart-healthy. Low fat. Whole-grain noodles." She was babbling.

When the horrifying thought sank in, she pressed her lips closed and ground her back teeth together. And oh, right, she was supposed to be flirting. So she batted her eyelashes.

"This is very nice of you." Will took the container she held out and met her gaze. Frowning, he asked, "Is there something wrong with your eyes?"

"Oh. No. I mean—" She blinked furiously. "I think there was something in one, but it's fine now."

"Good."

Doggone it! This flirting thing wasn't easy. It just felt

awkward and dishonest. She should cut her losses and run for cover. "Okay, then. I'll see you around."

"Come on in." Will moved the door open a little wider with his shoulder. "Unless you've got plans."

"No." Jean Luc was busy tonight, so she was free to flirt.

She walked into the house that was as familiar to her as her own. The door opened into the family room with a leather corner group and a flat-screen TV mounted on the wall. On the other side of a granite-covered bar was the kitchen with its large square island, stainless-steel appliances and plentiful oak cupboards.

She looked around. "It's awfully quiet. Where is everyone?"

"Kim is out with Luke." He set the casserole on the island and looked at her. The expression on his face said his sister and her fiancé weren't out so much as staying in and having sex.

April's already pounding pulse kicked up a notch. "What about your dad and Tim?"

"They went to a movie."

"Okay." The house was empty. In theory that worked for her plan except that she wasn't very good at flirting. "Well, then, now you have dinner. Enjoy."

He slid her a questioning look. "Have you eaten yet?"

"No."

"What are you doing for dinner?" he asked.

"Oh, I have a frozen thing in the freezer." She cocked a thumb over her shoulder, indicating the general direction of her house, freezer and the frozen thing.

Will leaned back against the countertop and folded his arms over his chest. The tailored long-sleeved khaki-colored sheriff's uniform shirt fit his upper body like a second skin. Matching pants showcased his flat stomach and muscular legs to male perfection. She was the one with a seduction plan, but if this was being in control, she'd be better off flying by the seat of her pants.

"So," he said, "you put in time and effort on this food and you're going to eat something that's been in a state of suspended animation for God knows how long?"

"Yeah, pretty much. I do it all the time." She could have bitten her tongue clean off for saying that. How pathetic did it sound that she often ate by herself? Next he'd be asking how many cats she owned.

"Not tonight you won't," Will insisted. "You're going to stay and have some of the meal you made."

Per the plan she had to strike the right balance between reluctance and giving in. It wouldn't do to appear too eager. The problem was that having dinner with him was tempting and it was awfully darn difficult to tamp down her enthusiasm. Because, gosh darn it, she did eat alone most of the time and the prospect of companionship at a meal was awfully appealing. And she told herself any companion would do. Herself almost bought into that thought.

"I don't know—"

"Did you put poison in the casserole?"

"Of course not. Wow, you can take the detective out of Chicago, but you can't take the suspicion out of the detective."

"And you didn't put a gallon of hot sauce in there to sabotage it and get even with me?"

"It was for your dad. I didn't even know you'd be here. The goal is to make Hank stronger and *not* give him another heart attack."

"So stay. It smells pretty good. Have dinner here." His blue eyes darkened with challenge while the beginning of a grin curved up the corners of his mouth.

"If that law-enforcement thing hadn't worked out, you'd have made a pretty persuasive lawyer." She happened to be looking at him and saw the shadows cross his face. They were there for a moment, then disappeared. "I'd like that."

"How about a glass of wine?"

"Sounds good." It actually sounded fabulous, but again, balance. Not too eager.

He opened the refrigerator and pulled out a bottle of Chardonnay, then found two wineglasses in the cupboard. After removing the cork, he poured and handed her a glass.

"Can I help with something?" she asked. "There should be a touch of a green. I could throw some salad together. Microwave some broccoli."

"Yeah, broccoli would be easiest. But I can do that. You've already done more than your fair share."

"Can I at least set the table?"

"If you insist." He'd already opened the freezer and glanced over his shoulder at her.

The look zinged right through her. "I do."

"Okay."

April was here so often she knew where everything was stored. So she got out plates, utensils, napkins and water glasses, then arranged them all on the round oak table in the nook. She and Will moved around the kitchen as if this meal was a meticulously choreographed ballet. But instead of dips, twirls and lifts, they managed to avoid even the slightest touch. Was he on edge, too?

She put hot pads out, then took the casserole from the food warmer and set it in the center of the table with a serving spoon. The bubbling had stopped but the dish was still warm and smelled yummy if she did say so herself.

Will set a steaming bowl of broccoli beside the noodle dish and said, "Let's eat."

April sat across from him, then put food on her plate and dug in. Macaroni and cheese was world-class comfort food, but noodles and chicken came in a close second to her way of thinking. Since Will had come back to Blackwater Lake, comfort was in short supply. Now here she was sharing a meal with him and feeling decidedly *un*comfortable.

"I can't remember the last time we had dinner together," she said.

Will took a sip of wine, then his mouth pulled tight. "I'm sorry, April."

"The thought just popped into my mind. I didn't say that to make you feel bad," she assured him.

"I know. And yet I do." He toyed with the stem of his glass, those big hands dwarfing the delicate crystal that had been his mother's. "I should have told you that I was dating someone. It was a lie of omission and I'm not proud of how I handled it."

April put down her fork and picked up her wine, then took a sip. He was sincerely sorry about what happened and that confused her. The goal was to seduce him and be the one to walk away, but this contrite Will made her question the mission. It was for closure, she reminded herself. That didn't mean she couldn't meet him halfway.

"Look, Will, it takes two to make a relationship. You're not the only one responsible for the way things turned out. If you remember back, communication between us had dropped off by a lot. You're not entirely responsible for that. Phone calls and messages go both ways and I didn't hold up my end of that either."

"Still, I should have—"

"Let it go. Really. Do whatever you need to in order to work through this because I don't see you as good martyr material."

"No?" His mouth twitched.

"Let's file it under 'Not meant to be.' Thinking about that time and wondering what if will drive you crazy." She shrugged. "We'll never know what might have happened if my mom hadn't gotten sick."

"I suppose."

"No supposing," she said. "It's true. That part of our life is in the past. But this is a new time. Maybe there's a chance to salvage a friendship."

"I'd like that." He held up his glass. "To being friends."

She touched the rim of her glass to his. "Friends."

They drank, then smiled at each other. She might be a flirting failure but friends was a start. She could work with that.

Sometimes it was hard for Will to believe he was filling in for his father as the sheriff of Blackwater Lake. Granted it had been less than a week, but that didn't change the fact that he had big shoes to fill. Hank Fletcher had always been his hero and Will wanted to follow in his dad's footsteps. Any law-enforcement job was a big one, but compared to what he'd seen in Chicago, this gig was like maintaining order in the land of Far, Far Away.

The office had one main room with a couple of desks for a single deputy and the dispatcher/clerk. Clarice Mulvaney was in her midfifties, a plump, brown-eyed brunette, friendly and efficient. Deputy Eddie Johnson was Will's height, but skinny. He was barely twenty-one but looked about twelve. Or maybe that was just because Will felt so old. Still the kid was smart and eager to learn.

In the back of the room there was a door that led to two six-by-eight-foot cells, empty at the moment and since this was Tuesday there was a very good chance they would stay that way. Things got a little extra exciting on the weekend when someone was more likely to be drunk and disorderly. Although every day was a weekend now because the official kick-off of summer had been last Saturday. So there was no taking weeknights for granted with tourists all over the place for the next three months.

As acting sheriff, Will took the private office off to the right, which had a closing door. Rank had its privileges.

The phone rang and Clarice answered. "Blackwater Lake Sheriff's Office. This is Clarice." She listened for a moment then said, "Is everyone all right?" After grabbing a pen, she jotted down notes. "Okay. Sit tight. I'll send someone right away."

"What's up?" Will asked.

"MVA on Lake Shore Road. Two cars involved."

Will moved in front of her desk. The sheriff also co-ordinated fire-department services. "Do we need to roll rescue and paramedics?"

"No. Everyone was out of the cars and there are no apparent injuries. But neither of the vehicles is drivable, so we need to alert McKnight Automotive that there will be either a tow or flatbed truck removal."

"Okay. Can you take care of that?"

"Sure thing."

"Eddie," he said to the blond, blue-eyed deputy. "Take the cruiser out there and evaluate the situation. Talk to everyone involved and make a report. Radio in with your recommendations."

"Yes, sir." In a heartbeat the kid was out of his chair and ready to go.

Will held out the keys, and the deputy grabbed them on his way out the door. It didn't escape his notice that the kid's smooth face barely required a shave. Must be a thrill to drive a cop car. If there was another call Will would take his SUV. He stood beside his dispatcher and both of them watched the deputy put on the cruiser's lights before pulling away from the curb. As he'd been trained to do.

Will knew Clarice had worked with his father for over

twenty years and was a valued member of the small department. Hank had always said she made him look good. When the resort was completed, the town was going to grow and law enforcement would have to keep up with it. Not his problem, he reminded himself. After the summer he was out of here. But his dad was going to have to deal with it and that would mean more stress. He would need dependable, dedicated employees.

"What do you think of Eddie?" he asked.

Clarice looked thoughtful for a moment. "He's a good kid. Coolheaded, smart, conscientious. Your dad has an eye for talent." She grinned. "After all, you're here."

"Not because of talent. It's the training."

"Could be both," she said. "And your dad figured Eddie could benefit from your experience and training."

"While I'm here." Will didn't want to give the false impression that he was staying for good and put a finer point on her statement.

"One day at a time." She had a mysterious Zen expression on her face.

"Right."

He was looking out the window and saw the door to the Photography Shop open and April walked out. She turned and locked up, then crossed the street and headed toward the sheriff's office. It was possible she was going somewhere else, but he hoped not. The sight of her lifted his spirits just like she'd done last night when he found her on his porch with a casserole in her hands. It wasn't fancy food but turned out to be the best dinner he'd had in a long time.

That had little to do with the cooking and everything to do with the company. Like every situation, he analyzed it and figured he'd enjoyed the evening because any lingering guilt about hurting her was gone. There were other things that kept him up at night but not her. At least not guilt about her, because he'd lost some sleep wondering if her mouth still tasted as sweet as he remembered.

April walked into the office and saw him standing by the dispatch desk. "Hi."

"Hey."

She looked at the older woman. "Hi, Clarice. How's the family?"

"Everyone is doing great."

"Are you a grandmother yet?" April asked.

"Sandy's due after Labor Day."

"I didn't know you were going to be a grandmother," Will said.

"Because you never asked." Her tone was only marginally disapproving. "She and her husband live in California, a suburb of LA. He's an attorney for a big law firm there. Sandy works at a preschool, at least until the baby's born."

"Congratulations," he said.

"Thanks, boss. By the way, I'll need some time off after she gives birth."

"My father will be back then. I'm sure he already has you covered and it won't be a problem." Then Will remembered she had a son, too. What was that kid's name? Oh, yeah. "How's Mark?"

"Good. I'm surprised you remembered his name." She hadn't missed the slight hesitation. "He's getting a doctorate in marine science from the University of Miami."

"Wow."

"Yeah. A nerd like his dad."

Will knew her husband taught chemistry at the junior college located about twenty-five miles from Blackwater Lake. Where April had gone to school. Damned if even after all this time he didn't still feel a twinge remembering that she hadn't gone with him to Chicago.

Will looked at her now. "So, April, how can we help you? Are you here to report a crime?"

She laughed. "More like crime prevention."

"Oh?"

"Yeah. Would you mind if we talked in your office?" The words were for him, but April gave Clarice a shrug that was part apology, part I-know-you-understand.

"I've got work to do," the dispatcher said.

"Okay. In my office, then." He turned and headed in that direction with April behind him. When they walked in the room he asked, "Do you want me to close the door?"

"Not necessary. I just wanted a little privacy for this conversation."

"Okay." He indicated the two chairs in front of the desk. "Have a seat."

"Thanks." She sat down and the wattage on her smile was probably visible from space. Plus she was doing that weird thing with her eyes again. "I could use your help."

"With what?"

"Crowd control. More specifically teenage make-out prevention."

"A little more information would be really helpful."

"Yeah. Sorry." She laughed again, but the sound seemed more nervous than anything else. "Every year just after school gets out the high school kids get together in that open field a half mile from the high school. The seniors who ruled the school pass on the power, symbolically of course, to the juniors, who are now incoming seniors."

"Okay. But why do you need official backup?"

"That's the thing. It's not official, not technically a school function, so no chaperones are required. But these are teenagers and extra surveillance is the smart way to go."

"Why are you doing the asking?" Apparently his guilt

wasn't completely gone because there was a part of him surprised that she would request anything from him.

"I take pictures that always make their way into the yearbook. It's an annual thing they do. Every year." She cringed. "I already said that, didn't I?"

"Yeah."

"The thing is, I don't want any of them having sex on my watch."

"I guess not." He couldn't stop a small smile.

"Glad you think this is funny."

"No, I don't."

"Yes, you do," she challenged.

"Maybe a little." He shrugged.

"Come on, Will, be serious. These kids are drowning in hormones and they're sneaky."

He remembered. Partly because there was something about April that made him feel like a randy teenager again. The reaction could have been because she mentioned making out and sex, but he didn't think so. It was all her. The playful ponytail, curves that had grown curvier with time and a mouth that would drive a saint insane.

"What time is this photo shoot?"

"Tonight. Eight o'clock. I know what you're thinking," she said.

"I don't think you do."

"You'd be wrong. You're thinking that it would be better to schedule this earlier in the evening before the sun goes down." She shook her head and pressed those plump lips together. Then she seemed to remember something and forced a big smile, followed by some eyelash batting. "The problem is that a lot of the kids have summer jobs and aren't available earlier. Not to mention that I have a business and later is better."

She was wrong. That wasn't what he'd been thinking.

His thoughts ran more along the lines of finding a secluded place to get *her* alone in the dark. "I see."

"I thought you would." Her eyes took on a pleading expression. "So, can I count on you?"

Will was conflicted about what to do. He didn't want to turn her down. This behavior of hers was surprising. First dinner last night and now a request for assistance today. She smiled a lot and did that weird thing with her eyes, which he didn't recall, but they'd toasted to friendship last night. And today she'd voluntarily come to see him and ask for assistance.

On the flip side, it probably wasn't a good idea to be out with her after dark, what with his mind going randy teenager on him. Still, the kids would be around and that would cool his temptation. Friends helped each other out.

"Okay. I'll give you a hand."

"Thanks, Will." She smiled again, but it was the first natural one since walking into his office. And it was a stunner.

He really hoped this wasn't a mistake.

Chapter Three

It was a beautiful night for taking pictures. April had her digital SLR camera on a tripod set up in the meadow and was snapping pictures of the outgoing senior class student-body officers passing a plastic toy torch. Someone held up a handmade sign that said "Class of 2017—we rule the school!" She stopped and scrolled through the images, then adjusted the shutter speed in order to make the shots clearer while allowing for the light from a full moon.

And speaking of that… She counted heads for the umpteenth time. There were supposed to be ten and she tallied eight. "Where did Trevor and Kate go?"

She looked at the group of teens and every single one looked guilty as sin. "Come on. You know my rules. No getting frisky and pairing off during this shoot. I know the seniors who just graduated don't care. But listen up seniors-to-be, if you want me to take pictures next year you'll tell me where they went. Otherwise this tradition will just be a sad memory."

April looked at them and they stared back at her without speaking. "Anyone? Now would be a good time to speak up. You really want to spoil the fun for the other classes coming up behind you?"

"You're right. We don't care." That was Mike Espy, a good-looking football player who'd received a football scholarship to the University of California, Los Angeles. "I can't wait to get out of this two-bit nowhere town. It's big-city excitement for me."

"Oh, don't be such a jerk." Patty Carnegie, a pretty blonde cheerleader who was looking forward to senior year and being captain of the squad, gave him a withering look. Then she met April's gaze. "They took a walk."

Red alert. That was code for finding a place to be alone and unleash all the teenage hormones raging through them. Will was out there somewhere. She knew because they'd come here together in his SUV. Part of her had expected him to back out, but he'd been right on time.

She wondered if he'd felt the same way Mike did about not being able to shake the dust of Blackwater Lake off his shoes fast enough. That didn't really matter now, though. She had two unaccounted-for teenagers who could be getting into trouble on her watch.

"Look who I found wandering around in the woods." And there was Will, walking the two wayward kids back to the group.

There was a lot of good-natured hooting and hollering but Trevor and Kate looked unrepentant. "We had to try," he said.

"And I have to tell you not to do it again."

April shot Will a grateful look. He shrugged as if to say he didn't blame them. Kids would be kids. She and Will had been there once upon a time when his father the sheriff had broken up one of their make-out sessions.

The windows of Will's seen-better-days truck had been fogged up and they felt like the only two lovers in the world. Right up until the moment there was tapping on the driver's door. April quickly adjusted her clothes and Will rolled down the window. Hank peeked inside and ordered him to get her home on time. She never knew if Will's dad had said anything to him privately. Hmm.

"Okay, you guys, let's finish up." April took her place behind the camera again.

"What should we do?" Lindsay was a junior and incoming student-body treasurer.

"Just be yourselves. Hang out. Pretend I'm not here," she advised.

"You just told us not to do that again," Mike reminded her.

Everyone laughed and she snapped a great picture. "I told you not to go walking alone in the woods. Now I want you to relax, have fun. If you think about getting your picture taken, you'll freeze up and be stiff. So act as if I don't have this camera trained on you to record this moment in the history of Blackwater Lake High School."

"Go Wolves," someone called out.

"Let's hear it for the blue and gold," a boy said.

Spontaneously the kids started a cheer. "Two, four, six, eight, who do we appreciate?"

"Kennedy," everyone hollered.

Then a chant started. "April! April! April!"

She smiled, watching them have fun. The innocence of youth that she was capturing forever. She got some great unstructured shots, more than enough to provide the yearbook committee with outstanding choices.

"Okay, you guys. Listen up. This is a wrap." She grinned at all of them. "Great job. Sheriff Fletcher will make sure everyone has transportation home."

A couple of the girls hugged her and expressed the appreciation of everyone, then hurried off with the group to the dirt area where they'd parked cars. Will brought up the rear and the moonlight allowed her to appreciate what a very excellent rear he had. That reaction was a direct result of pent-up big-girl hormones because she hadn't had a real date for a while.

She heard the sound of cars starting then driving away while beginning the task of packing up her equipment. It had been fun as always and her threat to discontinue future photo shoots was an empty one because she enjoyed it as much, if not more, than the kids. Maybe because her senior year in high school had been the happiest time in her life.

When the car noises faded she saw Will walking toward her. The anticipation filling her at the sight of him wasn't too much different than what she'd felt when they'd been together before. Flirting with a toad would be a challenge. But for the purposes of this plan to put him behind her, April knew it was good to be attracted.

"Mission accomplished." He watched her pack up her cameras and lenses and put them in their protective cases.

"Everyone got off okay?"

"Yes. And I have to say it was like herding cats."

"I know what you mean." She looked up at him and her heart stuttered. At some point she was going to have to get a handle on that reaction, but it probably wouldn't happen tonight. "Seriously, Will, thanks for your help. I'm really glad you were here for backup."

"I didn't do much."

"You did a lot. Not just anyone can stand there and look intimidating, but you pulled it off spectacularly."

"It's a gift. Then there were those two who just had to defy authority," he said.

"And you got them safely back to the herd. Bless you."

"Happy to help."

"I appreciate it." She had packed everything up while they talked and now folded the tripod. "I'm all set."

"Let me get that for you." He easily picked up everything that would have taken her two trips to haul.

"Thanks."

In silence they walked back to where his SUV was parked in the dirt area. He opened the rear liftgate and stowed her equipment while she climbed into the passenger seat. Moments later he slammed the door then settled behind the wheel and turned the key in the ignition. The dash lights illuminated his features and the past came rushing back to her. All the dreams, hopes and hurts of that teenage girl she'd once been.

One of the perks of not being together anymore was that theoretically she no longer cared what he thought of her. That meant she didn't have anything to lose by asking him whatever popped into her head. And she did it now. "Do you remember that night we were in your truck, parked right here, and your dad found us?"

"I wish I could say no." The glance he sent her was uncomfortable.

"Did he ever say anything more about it? When I wasn't there?"

"Yes."

She waited but he clammed up. "Care to elaborate?"

"If I said no would you let it drop?" This time he looked hopeful.

"From the perspective of a girl who never knew her father and missed that experience, it's my opinion that you should be grateful your dad cared enough to get involved. To risk alienating you."

"I get that now. At the time he really ticked me off."

"What did he say to you?"

"He told me not to disrespect you."

She smiled. "That sounds like Hank. Did he give you the don't-get-her-pregnant speech?"

"Don't remind me," he groaned, his reaction confirming her guess.

Considering they eventually broke up, it was a blessing there hadn't been an unexpected pregnancy. That reminded her of what Mike had said and she wondered how Will felt. This was as good a time as any to bring it up.

"Can I ask you something?"

"As long as it has nothing to do with my dad making me feel twelve years old."

"No." She laughed. "I don't know if you heard what one of the boys said. You were herding stray cats."

"What?" he asked.

"I said the graduated seniors probably didn't care but I was going to end the passing-the-torch tradition if they didn't follow my rules. He, Mike, confirmed that he didn't care and couldn't wait to get out of this small town, get a taste of the big city."

"Young and stupid," Will muttered.

"So you didn't feel that way when you were around his age?" she asked.

"No, I did."

"But you just said he's young and stupid. Do you regret moving to Chicago?"

He was quiet for several moments. "I just meant the big city isn't just about excitement." His mouth pulled tight for a second. "In a place with so many people there's a lot going on, both good and bad. The years give you perspective to see both sides."

"I guess so."

April had the oddest sensation of disappointment, as if she'd hoped he would admit he had regrets about leaving

Blackwater Lake, and her, behind. And wasn't that just silliness. It was a reminder of why she was here with him in the first place and romance was definitely not involved.

She'd foolishly believed that she and Will would be together always and deliriously happy. They would have kids and be the family she'd always longed for. He was right about years giving you perspective because she no longer had stars in her eyes. As far as she was concerned the only stars on her radar were in the sky and that's where they were going to stay. There was no way she would get sucked in to romance again.

Her assignment was to have a fling with Will and this time be the one to end things. High school had been happy because of Will, but now she had to put it, and him, behind her.

It was time for phase two of the plan. "Do you want to stop at Bar None for a drink? I'm buying. Call it a thank-you for your help tonight."

He didn't say anything for a few seconds and she braced for rejection. Finally he said, "That sounds good."

Here goes nothing, she thought. A friendly drink and that was it. She wasn't going to blow this chance for closure.

The morning after helping April with her teenage photo shoot Will was still trying to forget how beautiful she'd looked in the moonlight. And how eager he'd been to have a drink with her. There'd been a part of him hoping it would lead to more, but no such luck.

"You didn't have to come with me to see the doctor, Will."

"Hmm?" His father's voice pulled him back to the moment.

"I said, I could have brought myself here to the clinic. You didn't need to tag along."

"If I didn't, you know as well as I do that Kim's head would explode."

His dad laughed. He was sitting on the exam table in one of the patient rooms at Mercy Medical Clinic, waiting to see Adam Stone, the family-practice doctor on staff. Adam had consulted with the cardiologist and cardiothoracic surgeon who'd performed the bypass surgery and was now handling the follow-up checks. In fact, he'd stabilized Hank after the initial heart attack, before transport to the medical center in Copper Hill, which was over an hour away.

"Your sister *is* something of a control freak."

"That makes it tough when she can't be in two places at once." Sitting in a chair against the wall, Will grinned at his dad. "It was either doctor duty or her appointment with the manager at Fireside restaurant to consult on the food for her wedding reception."

"I'm glad she picked that one," Hank said. "This wedding is really important to her. And she's been through a lot of tough times. She's way past due for a chance at happiness."

"Yeah." Will couldn't agree more.

"The thing is, she would have put wedding prep on hold to come to this appointment with me if you weren't here, son." His dad's gaze was unflinching.

Will did his best not to squirm like a twelve-year-old in the hard plastic chair. Since coming back to Blackwater Lake it seemed guilt was his new best friend. His sister had carried all the family stuff, including being a teenage single mom while going to college and becoming a teacher.

And then there was April and how he'd treated her. At least he'd squared one out of those two guilt trips. She didn't seem to be holding a grudge about the past. He'd had a great time last night and it seemed as if she had, too.

Bygones went bye-bye. She was friendly and, if he didn't miss his guess, a little flirty.

Since that lightning-rod moment all those years ago when her full mouth and curvy body had grabbed him by the throat, she'd always had the power to get his juices going. As much as he wished that was a bygone, too, it had happened again last night.

But this doctor's appointment was about giving his sister a break so she could finalize details for her summer wedding.

"I'm happy to help, Dad." Will really meant that. "And I hope Kim enjoys everything—up to and including her wedding day. She deserves all the good stuff."

"Who's holding down the fort while you're here with me?"

Will had no doubt this was small talk because Sheriff Hank Fletcher still knew exactly what was going on in his jurisdiction. "Clarice and Eddie. They know how to get me if something comes up they can't handle."

"What do you think of Eddie? Professional assessment."

"Hard to tell. I haven't been here long enough to see him function in a crisis. But he seems bright, eager. He brings a lot of energy."

Hank nodded. "I thought so, too. Things are going to change when the resort and building development are finished. More people will move here, which is a blessing and curse. We'll do our best to anticipate potential problem situations but life has a way of throwing the unexpected at you just when you think you've got it all figured out."

Will didn't miss the sadness in his father's blue eyes and knew he was thinking about losing his wife in a car accident. He'd come home for the funeral but couldn't stay long. He had to get back to his job and proving himself to the seasoned veterans in the Chicago Police Department.

Or was that just what he'd told himself to shut down the guilt he'd felt for leaving the people he loved?

He and April had hooked up and it was the last time they were together. Considering they'd just buried his mother, it was probably the best and worst night of his life. She had made him forget the pain for a little while.

"It's good for Eddie to have you here," Hank said.

"Why?"

"You have a lot of big-city experiences. Blackwater Lake won't be on that scale, but there's a lot you can teach him that I can't."

"I'm happy to do what I can, Dad, while I'm here. But—"

There was a light knock on the door then it opened and the doctor walked in. In his white lab coat over light blue scrubs, Adam Stone greeted them both and shook hands.

"It's good to see you, Will."

"You, too." They'd met a couple months ago during his dad's health crisis.

"So, how's the patient doing?"

"Feeling great, doc." Hank pulled his T-shirt off as the doctor removed the stethoscope worn draped around his neck.

"Take a deep breath." Adam pressed the round thing to various places on his dad's chest and back, carefully listening each time he moved it. "Sounds good. Strong heartbeat and your lungs are clear."

He carefully inspected the scar on Hank's chest and nodded approval. "This looks awesome."

"Chicks dig scars," Hank joked.

"Then you should be very popular, Dad."

Adam laughed. "It's healing well."

"How's the wife and kids," Hank asked.

"Great. Couldn't be better." The doctor smiled broadly.

"C.J. is loving Cabot Dixon's summer camp and has decided he's going to be a cowboy when he grows up. Or Robin Hood. He's been taking archery classes with Kate Scott, actually Dixon now. They got married," he explained to Will. "And C.J. can't make up his mind whether he likes riding horses better than shooting a bow and arrow."

Hank laughed. "And that little girl of yours?"

"Beautiful. Just like her mom." His voice grew marginally softer when he mentioned the two women in his life. "Although I could do without the terrible twos. If she's as good at everything else as she is at that, she'll be incredibly successful in her chosen field."

"Yeah, I remember that stage," Hank said wryly. "My wife handled it and that's why Kim and Will grew up so well."

Will marveled at how his father got people to talk, to open up. He considered it part of his job to know the citizens of his town and the man was a master. That was very different from Will's work in Chicago. There was no way law enforcement could spend the time to get to know everyone.

Adam met his gaze. "How is it being back?"

Will figured he should be used to that question by now but it seemed every day in Blackwater Lake made his feelings a little less clear. So all he said was, "Good." Best to leave it at that and change the subject. "So my dad is doing okay?"

"Pretty remarkable actually. Pulse, heart rate, breath sounds, blood pressure are all where we want them. Anything you think I should know?" Adam asked.

"No. I'm feeling good," the patient said.

"I'm going to order some blood work."

"Heaven forbid I should get out of here without someone sticking me with a needle," his dad joked.

"Man up, Hank. You should be used to it by now," the doc said.

"Not really."

Adam glanced through the chart. "You're still exercising and watching your diet?"

His dad's expression was wry. "Have you met my daughter, Kim? You know, the pretty, bossy one?"

"Okay. Point taken. I'm betting that skill was sharpened by working with teenagers." Adam laughed. "I'll take that as a yes. So keep it up. At this pace you'll be ready to go back to work when your medical leave is over at the end of summer."

"Thanks, Doc."

"I want to see you again in six weeks. You can make an appointment with the receptionist on the way out." He shook hands with both of them again. "Take care."

Twenty minutes later they were in Will's SUV and headed home. After leaving the clinic his dad had grown unusually quiet, a stark difference from the gregarious man who was keeping up with the personal life of someone who lived in his town. The checkup couldn't have gone better. So what was the deal? Will was a police officer and trained detective but without clues he was unable to draw a conclusion.

And then there was this dandy technique that cops used to find out stuff. It was called interrogation. "What's going on, Dad? You're pretty quiet over there. The doc gave you high marks and said you'll be back to work soon."

"Yeah." The flat tone was a clue.

"Is this about work?"

"In a way. I've been thinking about retiring. I knew it was creeping up on me but didn't give it a lot of thought until the heart attack and surgery. Now…"

"What?"

"It's been on my mind. And you know that pretty, bossy sister of yours? She's been relentless about me slowing down. Taking it easy. Traveling."

"You've always wanted to," Will reminded him. "I remember you talking about it when Kim and I were kids."

"Not so much after your mom died."

Will felt a jab of guilt again that he hadn't been around much after the funeral. "I know that was a hard time for you."

"It was. And I'll always love her. But I'm not grieving the loss anymore." A big sigh came from the passenger seat. "Since Josie—"

"The widow who rents a room from Maggie Potter. I met her when you were in the hospital." Nice woman, he thought.

"Yeah. She stayed in Copper Hill to be there for your sister until I was out of the woods."

"I liked her."

"Kim does, too. And if she didn't—"

Will laughed. "It wouldn't be pretty."

"No kidding."

"You should take a trip," Will said. "With Josie."

"I'd like that, but I feel a responsibility to the folks here in Blackwater Lake. Can't just turn their welfare over to a rookie deputy, no matter how smart and eager he is. Not with the hotel and condos getting closer to opening every day."

"Yeah, I can see where you're coming from."

Will knew this was his dad hinting for him to make this temporary sheriff thing permanent. He remembered what that kid at the photo shoot had said about his hurry to get to the big city. In fact Will had told April he understood where the kid was coming from. But it felt like forever since he'd been obsessed with excitement, getting away from this town to do something more important.

"I know you do, Will. And I always knew you wanted me to be proud of your accomplishments. You have no idea how proud I am of you, the man you've become."

"Thanks, Dad."

"And you're older now. Age has a way of making you look at things differently. This town really has a lot to offer a man."

Just like that an image of sassy April Kennedy popped into his mind. She wasn't that skinny little girl anymore, but had grown into a beautiful, confident, accomplished woman. So many of his good memories were wrapped up in her, but she was the girl he'd left behind. It hadn't worked out for them and no matter what Will accomplished in his career the failure in his personal life would always bother him.

"Blackwater Lake was a good place to grow up. Tim is thriving here."

"Yes, he is. He's a great kid." There was grandfatherly pride in his voice, but there was something flat in the tone.

Will glanced over to the passenger seat and saw the look of resignation on his dad's face. He should have known the man wouldn't miss the way Will had deliberately changed the subject. There was no point in taking the idea any further. He would be going back to Chicago at the end of the summer.

That was just the way it was.

Chapter Four

In her kitchen, April peeked out her sliding glass door with its great view of Will's house across the alley. She knew he ran every morning and she did, too. In spite of Kim's dire prediction that she and Will were bound to run into each other, so far it hadn't happened. That was about to change. She hadn't seen him since he'd helped with the teenage photo shoot and that had been a couple days ago. The time had come to give her game a kick in the pants.

It was Sunday, the one day of the week that she didn't open the shop until afternoon. But she got up a little earlier than usual, put on her running clothes, stretched out and now watched the Fletchers' back door. If he didn't show soon she'd have to do her run solo and think of another way to get this flirtation show on the road. Then an ego-deflating thought hit her.

What if he just didn't like her at all?

Before she had a chance to blow that out of proportion

his rear door opened. It was him, and he leaned back inside for a moment. This was her chance.

She left the house and hurried up the sidewalk until reaching the alley, then pretended not to see Will, who stopped at the edge of the grass behind her.

"April?"

She glanced over her shoulder. "Hey, Will. Morning."

He caught up with her and fell into step. "Mind if I tag along?"

"Nope." It took effort not to look smug.

"How far do you go?"

"About six miles. Up Deer Springs to Spruce. Around the elementary school, down Elkhorn Road and back."

"Works for me."

She glanced over at him in his running shorts and snub gray T-shirt with the bold black letters *CPD* written on it. The wide shoulders and broad chest were pretty impressive and that was darned annoying. Why couldn't he be fat? Would it kill him to have male-pattern baldness setting in? But she wasn't that lucky. He was even better looking than when she'd loved him.

"Try to keep up," she said and increased her speed.

Will stayed right with her and it was easy for him because his legs were muscular and so much longer than hers. If he wanted to, he could leave her in the dust. But he didn't, so it wasn't a stretch to assume he didn't mind her company. She would go with that working theory.

"How's your dad?" She happened to look over at him and saw his mouth pull tight. "What's wrong?"

"He's fine." With the baseball hat and aviator sunglasses it was impossible to read his expression. "Had a checkup the other day and doc says he's the poster boy for how to recover from a heart attack."

"Oh, good. You scared me there for a minute." That was

a relief. Hank Fletcher was the father she'd never had. "It's just that you had a weird look on your face and I went to the bad place."

"Sorry. Didn't mean to send you there. Dad passed everything with flying colors. Doc even said if he keeps up the good work he'll get the green light to go back to the job at the end of summer."

"That's great." Then she noticed the muscle in his jaw flex and wondered what he was leaving out. "So why do you look like someone disconnected the siren on your cop car?"

He met her gaze and one corner of his mouth quirked up. "Because someone disconnected the siren on my cop car."

"Okay. Roger that. You don't want to talk about it."

April remembered a time when he told her everything, but obviously things had changed. It shouldn't bother her that he no longer confided in her. The fact that it did even a little was evidence that getting closure was the right way to go.

For about a mile they ran without talking. Then Will broke the silence. "How's business?"

"Good. Summer tourist traffic in the shop is up significantly from last year. Plus weddings keep me busy. 'Tis the season for them."

"Are you taking the pictures when my sister gets married?"

"Of course."

"But you're her best friend. Who's going to be her maid of honor?" Will asked.

"I don't think she's having one." She and Kim had sort of danced around this. If her friend had chosen someone else April would know. "I'm doing the bridal shower and everything the MOH is supposed to do before the actual ceremony. I'll just be too busy commemorating the important moments for posterity to actually take part in the important moments."

As they finished the loop around Blackwater Lake Elementary and headed back, Will asked, "Does it ever bother you to miss out on stuff because you're documenting memories?"

"I love what I do." If she missed out it wasn't because of taking pictures. People left her. Her father did before she ever knew him. Her mom died. Will… He found someone else.

"Now you're the one with a weird look on your face."

As their feet hit the asphalt in a rhythmic sound she glanced over, annoyed again. This time because he still knew her well enough to know when something bothered her.

"I have cramps," she said.

"Do you want to slow down? Walk the rest of the way?"

"No." She kicked up her speed again, enough that it kept them from talking.

April had done this route so many times she knew to start slowing down at the intersection of Deer Springs and Spruce. By the time they got back she was walking and stopped at the edge of her grass to stretch her muscles so she didn't really get cramps. Instead of saying goodbye, Will did his postrun stretching alongside her.

Again she couldn't help noticing how masculine he looked, his T-shirt showing darker spots around his neck and arms from the sweat. And, doggone it, that was sexy. If any health-care professional had checked her heart rate right then she could blame it on the run, but that would be a lie. The spike had nothing to do with exercise and everything to do with the Fletcher effect. It wasn't cause for alarm, just appreciation for a good-looking man. But it was still more evidence that she needed to ratchet up this flirtation in order to put him in her past where he belonged.

"Do you want a bottle of water?"

Will straightened slowly, clearly checking out her legs as he did. She was wearing a stretchy pink shirt over her sports bra and black spandex capris that fit her like a second skin. And she'd give anything to know if he liked what he saw. Darn sunglasses.

"I can throw in a cup of coffee," she offered, "and a muffin baked fresh this morning."

"Blueberry? Like you used to make?" There was a husky quality to his voice that amped up the sexy factor.

"Yes. Did that sweeten the pot?"

"Not really. You had me at water." He grinned. "But I wouldn't say no to a muffin."

That was why she'd made them. He'd always raved about her baking. If the spandex hadn't worked, muffins were her fallback strategy. The way to a man's heart through his stomach and all that.

"Come on in."

He followed her into the house, where she grabbed two bottles of water from the refrigerator, then handed one to him. He twisted the top off, then drank deeply, again one of those profoundly masculine movements that made her heart skip.

This was where she got it in a big way that the last time she'd kissed a guy had been longer ago than she could recall. The resulting knot of yearning wasn't a flaw in the plan, she told herself with a confidence that took some work.

"I'll turn on the coffee."

"Can I help?" He sat on one of the high stools at the bar separating kitchen and family rooms.

"No. Thanks."

Water and coffee grounds were ready to go; she only had to flip the switch. As soon as she did a sizzling sound started and almost instantly the rich coffee aroma filled the room.

"You've made some changes since the last time I was here," he commented.

"Yeah." She looked around the kitchen. This place was where she'd spent her teenage years. Now it was part of her inheritance, although she'd give it up in a heartbeat to have her mother back. "I updated the cupboards and changed the countertops to granite. Along with the house, my mom left me a little money and after I got the shop up and running there was enough left to do a few things."

"It looks good."

"I like it." She reached up into one of the cupboards and pulled out two mugs—one that said I Don't Do Mornings and the other sporting the Seattle city skyline, including Space Needle.

"Have you been to the Pacific Northwest?" he asked.

"Yeah. I went with a friend."

"Anyone I know?"

"Don't think so. Joe moved here after you left for Chicago." She poured coffee in the Seattle mug and handed it to him. "Do you still take it black?"

"Yup. Do you still drink yours the sissy way?"

"Of course. Cream and sugar." She smiled at the memory of how he used to tease her about this. "But these days it's nonfat and sugar substitute."

"Why?"

"A girl has to watch her figure."

"Some girls maybe, but not you. Guys will do that for you." Maybe it was wishful thinking but it sounded like there was a slight edge to his voice. "What does Joe do?"

"Construction. While he was here." She handed him a paper plate with a muffin on it.

"Does that mean he's gone?" He folded the cupcake paper down and took a bite of muffin.

"Yeah. He went back to Seattle. It's where he's from. We went there to visit his family."

"Do you keep in touch?" Definitely an edgy sarcasm in his tone.

"No." She poured cream in her coffee, then took the container and put it back in the refrigerator. When she turned back, she caught him staring at her butt and legs. And if her feminine instincts weren't completely rusted out, she was pretty sure he approved of what he saw. "There was no point. Long-distance relationships don't work."

"April—"

She held up a hand. "That wasn't a dig at you. Really, Will. It's just the truth."

He looked at her over the rim of his mug as he took a sip. "Okay." Then he glanced at his watch. "I have to get going. On duty in a little while."

"I guess peacekeeping is a seven-day-a-week job," she said.

"'Fraid so." He stood. "Thanks for the coffee and muffin. We'll have to do this again sometime."

"I'd like that." She walked him to the door. "Bye, Will."

"See you."

She watched him walk over to his house and remembered the approval on his face when he'd checked her out. A glow radiated through her and it wasn't just about the fact that her revenge plan was back on track.

No, this was about the fact that Will wasn't completely neutral where she was concerned. It was personally satisfying and she looked forward to more.

* * *

"I swear Luke and I are going to Vegas for a quickie wedding." Kim plopped herself down on the couch in the family room.

Will picked up the remote and muted the sound of the baseball game on TV. He'd only turned it on to keep himself from thinking about April. It wasn't working very well. The memory of her in those tight black running pants had his mind on things it had no business being on. The White Sox could wait. His sister, on the other hand, was on the verge of a meltdown if not already there.

"What's wrong?"

"Everything." She threw up her hands dramatically.

"Where's Dad?"

"At the movies with Tim. You're it, big brother. There's no one else here to deal with me. I don't need a big wedding. A small backyard barbecue would be perfect, don't you think? Or even something at the park. Easy peasy."

"You know you want a big wedding," Will reminded her.

"Why? What was I thinking?"

"That you've never been married before and you're only doing this once, so it's going to be a blowout affair."

"That's a direct quote, isn't it?" she asked.

"Yup." He looked at her beside him. "You said it the night before Dad had his surgery."

"Talk is cheap. Making a grand pronouncement is a lot easier than taking the steps to make it happen."

"Talk *is* cheap. But I can't help if you don't spit it out, Kimmie. What specifically is making you freak out?"

Tears welled in her blue eyes. "I got a call from the bridal shop. My dress is back-ordered and might not arrive in time."

"So pick out another dress." When big, fat tears started

rolling down her cheeks, he knew that was the wrong thing to say. "Hey, come here."

She slid over and leaned her head on his shoulder. "It's just…I w-wanted that dress."

"And it might be fine. Back-ordered isn't a definite *not going to happen*. But maybe you can pick out a runner-up just in case?"

"That's way too sensible." She sniffled and probably rubbed her runny nose on his T-shirt. "I just wanted to be bridezilla for a day. Throw a tantrum."

"And it was a beauty, sis. Way to be an overachiever." He put his arm around her shoulders and tucked her against him. "The thing is, I can guarantee that no one, including your groom, will know that any dress you wear is not your first choice."

"How can you be so sure?"

"Because you'd look beautiful in a burlap sack."

"Aw. That's sweet." She sniffled again and looked at him. "Makes me feel bad about blowing my nose on your shirt."

"It's yours now."

She smiled as intended. "How do you know Luke won't know it's a second-best dress?"

"Because guys don't care about that stuff. He'd be happy if you walked down the aisle naked." He winced. "I can't believe I just said that to my sister."

"It's okay. I took it in the spirit and all that. It's not a news flash that guys are pigs."

"That's harsh. We just have an acute appreciation for the female form."

"Right." She rubbed at an imaginary spot on the leg of her jeans. "Speaking of female forms, I saw you and April go running the other day and you went in her house when the two of you got back."

Will had forgotten how life was in a small town. Everyone watched what was going on and talked about it. At least Kim was talking to *him* and not someone at the Grizzly Bear Diner, which was ground zero for rumor spreading.

"So," he said narrowing his gaze on her, "your summer job while you're not teaching high school is doing covert surveillance for the CIA?"

"There are times when teaching teens feels like doing covert surveillance. It's not easy to stay one step ahead of those kids." There was a sly look in her eyes. "Speaking of steps, we were talking about you and April running together. What's up with that?"

"She runs. I run." He was having a little trouble concentrating after his naked woman remark, except April was the woman he was picturing naked. Okay, so he was a pig. He was a guy. He could own that. Because April had looked pretty spectacular in those tight black pants she'd worn. That spandex stuff hugged every curve and left little to the imagination, just enough that he wanted to take them off her and see everything. But that was pretty stupid, right? The two of them had their shot and he blew it. "I saw her in the alley before she started her run, so we went together."

His sister said something that sounded like, "Good for her," but Will couldn't be sure. "Afterwards she invited me in for coffee and a muffin."

"Is that what you crazy kids are calling it now?" There was a suggestive note in Kim's voice.

"There is no 'it.' We're friends. I guess."

"What does that mean?"

"I don't know." Will dragged his fingers through his hair. "It's just— When I made the decision to come back to Blackwater Lake for the summer, I knew I'd see her.

When you suggested I make sure the first time was private, I knew you were right. And—"

"What?"

"I was ready for it. I was prepared to deal with her anger. Possibly resentment. Hostility. Even hurt. I was braced for attitude whatever form it would take. That's something I'm trained to handle. After all, I'm Chicago PD."

Kim's forehead wrinkled. "What's your point?"

"My point is that I wasn't prepared for her to be friendly. She was a little resentful that first time I went over to her shop. But since then she's been—"

"What?"

"I don't know. So sweet my teeth are getting cavities."

"You've seen her a lot, then?" Kim looked like she was working hard at acting innocent.

"She brought over a casserole. Then asked for my help taking pictures of the graduating seniors passing the power torch to the incoming class. Before you say anything, I was working crowd control."

"Making sure no one had sex," she clarified.

He nodded. "We got a drink after. Her idea. Then we did our run together and had coffee."

"I still don't get the problem." Kim didn't look puzzled as much as a little self-satisfied. "It's all peace and serenity with your ex-girlfriend. Most guys would be ecstatic. Why are you complaining?"

"I'm not. Just the opposite."

"So, what is the opposite of complaining?" She tapped a finger to her lips. "Praise. Go into rapture over—"

"No one is going into rapture over anyone," he scoffed. "But she's acting pretty cool."

"You should have been more appreciative of what you had before sleeping with that woman."

"The only person you ever call *that woman* is my ex-wife, Brittany."

"Yeah. Her. And I bet she spells her name with an *i* at the end and the dot over it is heart shaped."

"Let me guess. You don't like her." Will knew exactly how his sister felt about his ex. She'd made it clear the first time they met.

Now Kim made a face that looked as if she'd taken a bite out of a sour lemon. "I never liked her."

"And I should have listened to you."

"It's very big of you to admit I was right, Will. I never thought the day would come when I'd hear you say those words. Although I was always aware that you felt like that."

"Don't let it go to your head. For what it's worth, on the divorce papers she spelled her name with a *y* and I assume that's the legal way. She wouldn't have slowed the process down by getting cute with spelling. She couldn't wait to be the ex Mrs. Fletcher."

"Don't tell me." Sarcasm was wrapped around every word. "She had her hooks into another guy. Probably seeing him before you two separated."

Although he had a whole lot of suspicion, Will had no independent facts to confirm it. All he said was, "Probably."

"You're well rid of her, Will." She put her hand on his arm. "Please don't let one bad experience make you gunshy about a relationship. After all, look at me."

"What about you?"

"I'm the poster girl for what not to do. Pregnant at seventeen and abandoned by the father."

"This isn't getting even, sis, but I never liked that guy."

"Okay. And I didn't listen to you. We need to work on that." She sighed. "But, my point is that I didn't close myself off from love and now there's Luke."

"You're a lucky girl." But this had to be said. "For the record, I'm a detective. I can track that jerk down if you want to get back child support out of him."

"Sweet of you, but no. Someday Tim might want to meet him or the jerk might want to see his son and if it feels right I wouldn't stop it. But if the guy asked my son for a kidney, he'd have to go through me." A fierce, protective, maternal expression settled on her face. "As of now I don't ever want anything from him. Things worked out for the best. Tim is a great kid."

"You'll get no argument from me."

Guilt, but no pushback. Not being there for her was one more thing to add to his list of sins. Will had gone ahead with his career and hadn't been around to support her. That kid of hers, his nephew, was terrific, because he had a terrific mom and a grandfather who was devoted to him.

Her face went soft as all teasing disappeared. "I keep wondering when he's going to show interest in the opposite sex."

"He might not show it yet, especially to his mom, but I guarantee you there's already interest."

Horror widened her eyes. "Should I talk to him about safe sex? I don't want him to make the same mistake I did and for sure I'd phrase it better than that because I don't for one minute consider him a mistake. He's a blessing. But I would much rather not have him be a father before he's out of high school. Or college, for that matter."

"Is there a health class in the high school curriculum?"

"Yes, but I'm his mom. I feel as if I should have a conversation with him. Shouldn't that come from me?"

"He won't want to hear it from his mom."

"Voice of experience?"

"Not exactly. Dad said something to me and I still didn't

want to hear it. That's just the way boys are." He met her gaze. "So, no one special for him yet?"

"He's only fourteen. Too young to date."

"I can talk to him about this if you want." Maybe make up for not being around when he should have been.

"Would you?" She hugged him. "Let him know I'm willing to have a conversation about anything he wants, but didn't want to embarrass him. And tell him that—"

"I'll let you write out the talk on five-by-seven cards if that would make you more comfortable," he teased.

She laughed. "No. Just make sure he's ready for anything when he starts dating. It's important for him, but he also has to protect any young woman he might be with."

"I'll make sure he understands." He cleared his throat. "Speaking of dates… April said she'll be taking pictures at the wedding."

"Yeah. She's the best. Even if I decide to have it in the backyard."

He ignored her little flare-up of nerves. "Is she seeing anyone?"

"She sees a lot of people. After all she has a business and works with the public—"

"I meant is she dating anyone?"

"Of course," Kim said. "She's really pretty and a lot of fun. Guys ask her out all the time. And there's this one. Jean Luc. He's a same-time-next-year ski instructor who's here every winter."

That information was more unsettling than Will had expected. The idea of her with another guy really bugged him. That was something of a surprise, even more than her being friendly.

"So no one right now?" he asked.

"Not that I know of." Again Kim had that overly innocent thing going on. "Why?"

"She tells you everything. What do you think about me asking her to dinner?"

Kim stood and looked down at him, possibly with pity in her eyes. "She's probably not interested, but you've got nothing to lose by asking."

"Okay, then."

"Now that I've let off steam, there are lists to make and stuff to plan." She started out of the room. "Good talk, Will."

"Yeah."

Maybe.

But he couldn't shake the feeling that Kim was wrong— and he had a lot to lose if April said no.

Chapter Five

April put the Back in an Hour sign in her shop window and locked the door. She glanced across the street for a possible Will sighting and was disappointed when she didn't see him. It hadn't been her habit to do that before he came back to town and she wondered how long after he went back to Chicago before she stopped.

That was concerning but fell into the question-for-another-day category. Right now she was going to see Kim. Her friend had called, announced she had some important news and insisted April meet her for lunch at the Harvest Café. Whatever she had to say, it needed to be shared in person and Kim had appointments all afternoon to deal with wedding stuff. Since they both had to eat, it was a two birds, one stone situation. Good thing all was quiet at the Photography Shop.

The café was two blocks away, so she turned right and curiosity made her pick up the pace. She couldn't imagine what was so important that Kim had to call an emergency meeting. Hopefully there wasn't anything wrong.

Main Street was busy with tourists window shopping and leisurely strolling the downtown area. When the new resort was completed with its hotel, condos and retail space, foot traffic would increase and she would have to think about hiring someone part-time. It was an exciting thought.

Almost as exciting as having Will in her kitchen discussing the fact that he thought other guys liked her figure, which, in translation, meant he'd at least noticed and approved. He'd asked more than one question about an old boyfriend and sounded just the slightest bit jealous. That was good. For the plan.

Except that was the thing. After she'd "accidentally" run into Will, the plan never entered her mind again when she was with him. She behaved naturally and enjoyed hanging out with him. No flirting. No skullduggery or underhandedness. Just friendly and fun. She was no actress and trying to be one made her uncomfortable.

She crossed the street with the Grizzly Bear Diner on the corner. It specialized in burgers and sandwiches. After that she passed Tanya's Treasures, a gift and souvenir shop that was now under new ownership. Tanya had moved to Southern California to be with a man, a tourist, she'd met here in town. Way to go, Tanya.

Next door to the gift shop was Potter's Ice Cream Parlor and then the Harvest Café, both owned by Maggie Potter and her business partner, Lucy Bishop.

April nearly ran into another passerby while drooling over the pictures of ice cream sundaes and fighting the urge to go in. Who needed a healthy lunch? But she could still hear her mother's voice in her head—dessert after you finish your dinner. It made her feel as if her mom was still with her.

She walked into the café, which was full of people sitting at the counter and tables scattered around the open room. The decor was country cozy and done in fall shades, with flowered tablecloths and color-coordinated napkins in gold, green and rust. A shelf high on the wall held a copper teakettle, tin pitcher, pottery bowls and dried flowers. The women of Blackwater Lake loved this place and dragged their significant others in frequently.

In fact, just inside the door, Maggie was there with Sloan Holden.

"Hi, April." Maggie was a pretty, brown-eyed brunette who now had a ginormous diamond on her left ring finger. "Have you met Sloan?"

"Yes," he answered for her. "Liam and I were in the Photography Shop looking at cameras. It's nice to see you again." He was a tall, handsome man. And nice.

"You, too." His son was about ten or eleven, April recalled, a polite, curious and funny kid. That said a lot for the dad's parenting skills.

"Kim Fletcher told me you're taking the pictures at her wedding in August. When Sloan and I started talking about setting a date for our wedding he mentioned the photos he saw in your shop." Maggie looked up at him and smiled. "We both want you to handle the photography for ours."

He nodded. "The wedding pictures I saw were really stunning, an excellent representation of your work."

"Thank you," she said. "I'd love to. When you pick a date let me know so I can block it off on my calendar."

"Will do." Sloan looked at his bride-to-be. "I hate to leave, but work is waiting."

"Me, too." She stood on tiptoe and kissed him. "I'm glad you came in for lunch. See you at home."

"Can't wait." Tenderly, he ran a finger over her cheek. "Bye. Nice to see you again, April."

"You, too."

The two of them watched him leave and April wanted to sigh right along with Maggie. She'd been a widow with a young daughter for several years before Sloan rented a room at her bed-and-breakfast. The two fell in love and now they were getting married. She'd gotten a second chance at happiness, and who didn't love a happy ending?

April was only human and couldn't help just the tiniest bit of envy that crept in. She'd fallen in love once upon a time. But a happy ending? Not so much.

Maggie snapped out of it and looked at her. "You're meeting Kim Fletcher, right? She's already here. That table back in the far corner."

April spotted her friend who gave her a wave. "Thanks, Maggie. And let me know about that wedding date."

"Will do."

She picked her way through the full tables, then sat down across from her friend. "Hi."

"Hey, kiddo. Glad you could meet me."

"You said it was important. Is your dad okay?"

"The doctor says he's doing great."

"Will told me." She remembered the look on his face when he'd relayed what the doctor had said. There was something going on with him and his dad, but he'd changed the subject. Still, that had been a couple days ago. "Has there been a setback in Hank's recovery?"

"Not if he knows what's good for him," Kim said fiercely. "And I make sure he does."

"No kidding. You're bossy in the best possible way."

"That's what Luke says."

April hoped there wasn't a hiccup in the relationship and that was the reason for this meeting. "How is your guy?"

"My guy," her friend said dreamily. "Makes me want to burst into song. But don't worry. I know my limitations. No one wants to hear that."

"I think you have a lovely voice," April said loyally.

"That's why I love you." Kim turned serious. "And speaking of love…"

"Oh, God. Who else is engaged?" Not that April didn't like a romance as much as the next person, but this town was swimming in it.

"What does that mean?"

"Let me recap." April held up her fingers to count off the couples. "You and Luke. Maggie and Sloan, who just asked me to take pictures at their wedding. His cousin Burke and Sydney McKnight. Her father, Tom, married the mayor. Then there's Cabot Dixon and Katrina Scott, the runaway bride. They're all recently married or engaged. It's an epidemic. Or something in the water."

No, scratch the last one. If that were the case, April wouldn't feel like a slacker.

"Don't worry, sweetie. Your time will come. The biggest problem you'll have is who's going to take pictures at your wedding since you won't be able to do it yourself, what with being the bride and all."

"You don't have to say that, Kim. I don't need a man in order to be fulfilled." That was true, but she'd loved being in love. "I have my business. In fact I'm thinking of hiring someone part-time."

"That's wonderful. But you don't have to choose between the two. A woman can have a career and a relationship."

April had no doubt that was true except she'd all but given up hope of having both in her life. And that was okay. She'd gone along with this plan in order to have closure. "You didn't call me here for a pep talk. What's up?"

"I'm pretty sure my brother is going to ask you out."
Kim waited for a reaction and when one wasn't forthcoming, she looked a little disappointed. "I expected a screech.
A smile. Something."

April's heart skipped and stuttered, but the other woman
couldn't see that. "How do you know this?"

Before Kim could answer, their waitress appeared.
"Welcome to the Harvest Café. What can I get for you
ladies?"

"We're kind of in a hurry. I really hate to do that to
you," Kim said. "But I have appointments and April has
to get back to work. So, I'd like an iced tea and the cranberry Cobb salad."

"Make it two." April handed over her menu.

"Coming right up."

"Okay," April said when the young woman was gone.
"How do you know he's going to ask me out?"

"He told me. Practically."

"What does that mean?" This felt a lot like junior high,
but April couldn't seem to shut off the need for details.

"He was asking questions. Like are you dating anyone.
And I said of course you were since you're gorgeous and
smart." Kim took a breath. "Then he put a finer point on
it and wanted to know if you were exclusive with anyone,
so I told him about Jean Luc, your winter-ski-instructor-
lover. Same-time-next-year sort of thing."

"There is no Jean Luc."

"He doesn't know that." Kim's grin was wicked. "He
didn't look happy."

Was it wrong, April wondered, that inside she was
pumping her arm in a gesture of triumph? "Then what?"

"He asked what I thought about him inviting you to
dinner."

"And you said?" April held her breath.

"I told him you probably wouldn't be interested, but he had nothing to lose by asking."

"You didn't." Of course she was interested.

"Yes, I did. You don't have to thank me."

"Good, because I wasn't planning to. What if I am interested?"

"Of course you are. That's what this plan is all about in the first place." Kim stopped when the waitress brought a tray with their salads and drinks, then set everything on the table.

"Anything else I can get you?"

"Just the check," Kim said.

"You got it."

April picked up her fork. "So you don't really know if he's going to ask."

"Oh, he is," her friend said confidently. "And when he does, you need to play hard to get."

"Wait a minute. Isn't this the goal?"

"Well, sleeping with him is the goal, but this is a start. But it shouldn't be too easy. Not only would that make him suspicious, men never appreciate anything they didn't have to work for." Kim took a bite of her salad.

"I don't know," April said. "And I already asked him to go for a drink after he helped me out."

"That doesn't count. And this way you'll keep him guessing. Trust me, sweetie. The end will be much more satisfying if you string him along just a little."

"Look, Kim, you know me better than anyone. You know I don't play games." She pushed the greens topped with dried cranberry, egg, bacon, blue cheese crumbles and avocado around the bowl. "The thing is I want to go out with him. Pretending makes me uncomfortable. Don't you think it's time to just be up front with Will?"

"Absolutely not." Kim gave her a don't-you-dare look.

"Remember why you're doing this in the first place. If you play this my way, everyone in Blackwater Lake will be talking about you and Will."

"But we had our chance and it wasn't meant to be," April protested.

"Did I say anything about my brother proposing?" She shook her head. "I did not. This is all about you moving on. That's going to happen when you get a chance to tell Will that you're not into him. Do you trust me, April?"

"Of course I do. You're the sister I never had. I know you wouldn't steer me wrong."

"Darn straight." Kim smiled. "This is going to work. I just know it."

April hoped she was right. She wanted to put Will Fletcher behind her before he went back to Chicago and put Blackwater Lake behind him.

Will had forgotten what a Blackwater Lake Fourth of July was like.

The shops in town were dripping with red, white and blue decorations. American flags flew on lampposts and residences. There had been a morning parade on Main Street with horses, cars, wagons and kids from elementary to high school. The town fire engine was the finale. Every parade entry was decorated for Independence Day and prizes were awarded for the most artistic, innovative and patriotic. Mayor Goodson-McKnight had picked the winners.

About two o'clock folks started showing up at the park for games of touch football, soccer and water balloon tosses that got fairly rowdy in a wet way. People staked a claim to the park tables by the built-in barbecues, where the town council and volunteers grilled hamburgers and hot dogs.

Blankets and chairs were spread out and arranged under trees as a break from the sun, also keeping in mind the best vantage point for the upcoming fireworks display put on by the fire department. That would happen in about an hour. The whole scene was like a long, cold beer for the small-town patriotic soul.

Being on duty here was, well, a walk in the park compared to a shift in Chicago on this holiday.

Will had seen April turn up everywhere with a camera hanging around her neck and a pocket-sized notebook in her hands. She was alternately taking pictures and getting names of the folks she'd snapped to document the festivities for the *Blackwater Lake Gazette*.

She was the picture of patriotism in her denim shorts, red-and-white-striped spaghetti-strapped top, hair pulled back in a perky ponytail. And he found himself on the alert, constantly watching for those particular denim shorts and top. Her shapely, tanned legs tied him in knots, especially because he remembered how good it felt to have them wrapped around his waist while he was buried deep inside her.

Will snapped his attention back to his job and picked his way through tables, blankets and toddlers, watching for any potential trouble that could mar the celebration. Then he heard his name and recognized Cabot Dixon, a local rancher who also ran a kids' summer camp.

He walked over and shook hands with the man, who stood up. "Been a long time, Cabot."

"Yeah." He indicated the pretty woman beside him with the light brown, sun-streaked hair. "This is my wife, Katrina Scott."

"It's Kate Dixon now." She smiled. "Nice to meet you, Sheriff."

"Will," he said. Pieces of stories he'd heard fit together.

"You're the woman who showed up at the Grizzly Bear Diner in a wedding dress."

"Guilty. I don't suppose I'm ever going to live that down," she said, not looking the least bit bothered.

"Probably not," Will agreed. "It's one of those legends that will be passed on from generation to generation and immortalized with a hammer and chisel on cave walls."

"I was sort of hoping for a Facebook fan page," she teased.

"She's the best thing that ever happened to me." Cabot put an arm around her shoulders and pulled her in closer to him. "Other than Tyler, of course."

"How old is your son now?"

"Going on ten. He's over there." Cabot pointed to a group of boys in an open grassy area playing soccer. "I heard you were the new sheriff in town."

"*Acting* sheriff. It's temporary." No matter how much his dad might want him to be permanent.

His friend looked around the idyllic setting. "This must be really different from Chicago. Will is a detective with CPD," he explained to his wife.

"It's the polar opposite of what I'm used to," Will agreed.

"Must be boring here," Cabot guessed.

"Excitement can be highly overrated." He shrugged. "I keep busy. Today alone I've confiscated enough illegal fireworks to take out a good-sized city."

"Teenagers?"

"Of course." He grinned and his friend returned it. "We did our share of that when we were their age."

"And your dad always caught us."

"Every year," Will confirmed.

"You guys tried it more than once?" Kate's blue eyes went wide.

"It was worth a shot," Will and Cabot said together.

"Men." She shook her head. "They get bigger but never stop being little boys."

"It's basic training," her husband explained, brown eyes teasing. "When Ty gets to be a teenager, he won't be able to get away with anything because I've done it all."

"My nephew complains about that. And he's living with two cops. He'll have to be twice as good as we were to be even half as bad."

"If they're going to pull stuff, and they are," Cabot said, "at least there's a lot less trouble to get into here in Blackwater Lake."

He and Kim had turned out okay and her son was doing great, Will thought. "I suppose it's a good place to raise kids."

"Sure hope so." Cabot looked at his wife who nodded slightly. "Just found out we're having another one."

"Congratulations." Will shook the other man's hand again. He saw the expression of pleasure, pride and excitement on his friend's face and felt a stab of envy.

"We're very excited," Kate said. "Ty is going to be a wonderful big brother. Although he's very vocal about not wanting a sister."

"I know how he feels. Mine's been a pain in the neck since she was born," Will teased.

"You don't mean that," she said.

"You're right. Kim is the best and that reminds me. Her son is fourteen and I need to make sure he's not doing what Cabot and I would have been doing at his age."

Cabot laughed. "Good luck with that. It was really great to see you again."

"You, too."

Will walked away and found his nephew shooting hoops with some friends while a group of teenage girls watched.

Judging by the hormone-drenched looks going back and forth between Tim and one of the young ladies, the talk Will had promised to have with the kid should happen pretty soon, he thought.

Keeping his eyes and ears open, he moved through the crowd, saying hello to old friends and being introduced to recently relocated residents. Learning what was going on. Sydney McKnight was engaged to Burke Holden, who was involved in building the new resort up on the mountain. His cousin and business partner, Sloan, was engaged to widow Maggie Potter. Her brother, computer millionaire Brady O'Keefe, had married his executive assistant.

Envy hit him again, smacked right into him like a bug on a windshield. Perspective was a funny thing. He'd run to something for his career and somehow felt as if he'd been left behind. He figured that feeling was as temporary as filling in for the sheriff.

Keep moving, he thought, making another circuit through the park. He was nearing the parking lot and saw the fire department's red hook-and-ladder truck parked there. In preparation for the holiday, he'd coordinated with fire and rescue to mobilize for the community celebration in the park. There was always a chance that Will would miss confiscating some banned fireworks and they could escalate into a big blaze during the dry summer months. Or someone shooting them off could get hurt.

Walking closer, he saw the fire captain he'd worked with. Desmond Parker. Nice guy who'd been recruited from Lake Tahoe, California, to expand the department as necessary to deal with the resort development.

He looked closer and saw that Des was chatting up a woman in a familiar red-striped, spaghetti-strapped knit top and denim shorts. It was April and she was smiling. Worse, she was looking at the guy the way she'd looked at Will when they were at Bar None, as if she was having a good time.

That started a slow burn in his gut and no high-powered fire hose was going to put it out.

Will stepped off the curb, onto the parking lot asphalt, and walked over to them. "April."

She looked pleased to see him just before her expression shifted into neutral, as if she'd caught herself and dialed down the reaction. "Hi, Will."

He held out his hand to Des. "Good to see you."

"Happy Fourth."

"You two know each other?" April looked at him, then the other man.

"We met at a community preparedness planning meeting," Des explained.

"Oh. Right," she answered. "Of course you would.

Will was no expert on what women found attractive in a guy, but he could see where this particular one could appeal. He was tall, blue eyed and sandy haired with a strong jaw and muscular build. Then there was the dark blue pants and shirt making up the uniform. He knew from personal experience that women liked the uniform.

And damn it. He hadn't sized up a guy like this since... Hell, ever. Even worse, he actually liked Des Parker. He was a stand-up guy and knew his job, but the thought of April with him was infuriating. Will knew why. He was jealous.

"How's it going?" Will asked him.

"So far, so good. On your end?"

"Quiet. I've got a lot of unauthorized pyrotechnics in the trunk of the cruiser. I'll turn them over to you tomorrow."

Des grinned. "The guys and I will have fun getting rid of them."

Will knew they were going to shoot them off. The difference was firefighters knew how to take the necessary precautions and do it safely. He couldn't stop a reluctant smile. "I'm sure you will."

Des looked at his watch. "Speaking of shooting off fireworks, I have to go. We're staging for the town's display now."

"Let me know if you need any help," he offered.

"Will do."

"Thanks for letting me get some photos of you with the truck, Des."

"Anytime." The other man smiled at April. "I'll call you."

"Okay."

Watching the man walk away, Will wished there was some town ordinance prohibiting a guy he actually liked from hitting on another guy's ex-girlfriend. But if that was the case, the sheriff's department would need a lot more deputies.

Alone at last, he thought, looking at April. Was he the only one who felt something simmering between them? Detectives were trained and on-the-job experience sharpened gut instinct about people. He didn't think she was disinterested and it was time to find out if he was right.

"You've been busy today. Taking pictures, I mean."

"Yeah. People enjoy seeing themselves in the paper." She glanced at the crowd in the park. "I should go set up to get some pictures of the fireworks."

"Before you go, there's something I'd like to ask you." Will realized he was nervous. He hadn't been nervous asking a woman out since he was a little older than his nephew.

"Yes?"

"We could both use some R & R after a busy day. I was wondering if you'd like to have dinner with me tomorrow night."

She looked at him for several moments. "It's very nice of you to ask. But I don't think so."

"Okay." He was about to ask for an explanation, but she turned away.

"I have to go."

Will stared at the sway of her hips as she walked toward where the whole town was gathered. Well, slap him silly if that didn't make him hotter than a sparkler even though she'd just rejected him.

Women, he thought, were beyond the understanding of mortal men. Detective skills were not useful in unraveling the mysteries of a woman's mind and that was damned unfair.

Chapter Six

"What's all this crap?" Will had just rolled out of bed and headed downstairs for coffee. Now he stared at the mound of files and paperwork that covered every square inch of the kitchen table. He gave his sister, who was sitting in front of it, a patented Chicago PD glare.

She didn't look the least bit intimidated. "This, dear brother, is my wedding. Files for every phase from reception menu to flowers. Receipts, invoices and samples that combined will make it a perfect day."

He was not in the mood for perfect anything, especially a wedding. Yesterday April had turned him down flat. It wasn't ego talking. Okay, maybe a little. But more troubling was that he might be losing his edge. He couldn't believe he'd read her so completely wrong.

Leaning his back against a counter with his arms folded over his chest, Will wasn't ready to let this drop. "How is a guy supposed to sit at the table and eat breakfast? And forget about opening a newspaper to read."

"Stand up and eat cereal the way you usually do," she snapped back.

There was nothing she could do to make him admit she was right about his normal pattern. "What about the other people in this house who might want to sit down to a leisurely meal?"

"Dad went somewhere with Josie. And Tim isn't up yet." She glared right back at him. "You're certainly in a mood."

"This isn't a mood. This is an attempt to stand up for male freedom and equality in this house. We have a right to use the table. The good of the many outweighs the good of the one."

"Oh, for Pete's sake. This won't be forever. Just a few more weeks then I'll be out of your hair."

"It won't matter then. I'm going back to Chicago right after that." Without getting a chance to spend time with April. That realization did not improve his mood.

"What's wrong?" Kim studied him intently.

"Nothing."

"Come on. This is me. Does your mood have anything to do with April?"

His gaze snapped to hers. "Why?"

"That was just a shot in the dark but I obviously got it right." Her eyes narrowed on him. "You asked her out and she said no."

"She told you."

"No. I swear."

His people radar was malfunctioning and he couldn't be sure, but she looked just a little too innocently sincere. "She must have said something to you."

"I haven't seen her since yesterday at the town picnic in the park," Kim vowed.

"She could have called. You two are BFFs. You tell each other everything."

"Yes. But this is breaking news. She didn't tell me she shut you down."

He winced. "Way to make me feel better."

"I'm sorry, Will."

"Go ahead and say I told you so." Kim had also told him he had nothing to lose by asking but it didn't feel that way right now.

"I would never do that. Not when you're so upset."

"I'm not upset. Why would I be? It's no big deal. April and I are friends and I thought it would be a good idea to hang out. She didn't want to. I'm over it."

"Epic shutdown, Uncle Will." Tim walked into the kitchen wearing a gray T-shirt displaying in black letters *Blackwater Lake High School Football*. His hair was sticking up and there was enough stubble on his jaw to prove he was closer to fifteen than fourteen. Clearly he'd overheard that April had said no. And now he was staring at the table where his mom was sitting. "What's all this crap?"

"That does it." Kim gave them both the hairy eyeball, then let her hostile gaze rest on Will. "You barely know your nephew. Take him and go do something."

"Are you throwing me out?" Will asked.

"Look at it as an opportunity to bond."

Tim backed away. "I think we better do what she says, Uncle Will, or her eyes will turn red and her head might explode."

"Yeah, kid. Sounds like a plan."

Looking like two rejects from a suspect lineup, they left the house. After stopping at the Grizzly Bear Diner for take-out breakfast sandwiches, Will drove out to the Blackwater Lake Marina.

"Do you like fishing?" he asked his nephew.

"It's okay."

"Let's rent some gear at the marina store."

"Cool."

They walked in and looked around. There were circular racks of T-shirts and lightweight outerwear. A cold case against the wall was packed with soda and water with a display case of chips and snacks beside it. Another wall held fishing equipment from poles to lures. Will recognized Brewster Smith standing behind the cash register at the checkout counter. The man had worked there as long as he could remember.

"Hey, Brew."

"Will Fletcher." This guy was close to sixty if he hadn't already rung that bell. He had a full silver beard and a head of hair to match. "I was wondering how long it would take you to get out here. Heard you were back."

"Temporarily. Are you ever going to quit this job?"

"Nope."

"I'm sure Jill Beck appreciates your loyalty."

"Don't work for her anymore. And she's Jill Stone now. She married a doctor from Mercy Medical Clinic and had a baby girl. They sold the property, marina and all, to a famous writer fella and built a big house in that fancy development overlooking the lake."

"Who's the writer?"

"Jack Garner."

"No kidding?" Will had read his book *High-Value Target*. It was a big hit. Spent months at the top of the bestseller lists.

"Yeah, but I don't see him around much. He keeps to himself."

"Must be working on the next book."

"I guess." Brew grinned at Tim. "Hey there, young fella. Been a while since I've seen you out here with your grandpa. How's he doing?"

"Good. Thanks for asking, Mr. Smith."

"Glad to hear it." The older man rested his hands on the counter and looked at them. "What can I do for you?"

"Do you still rent fishing gear?" Will asked.

"Sure do. I'll fix you fellas right up."

The man was as good as his word and fifteen minutes later they had set up at the lake's edge and were sitting side by side in folding chairs that had holders for their fishing poles while waiting for a fish to bite. Their lines were in the water. The sky overhead was a perfect shade of blue and the sun was shining. Uncle and nephew ate their breakfast in silence.

Will figured he was the adult and it was up to him to break the silence that was growing more awkward by the second. When nothing that wasn't lame came to mind he realized two things. First, Kim was right about him not knowing his nephew. Second, the only kids Will had contact with were in trouble with the law. If Tim had been caught stealing or with an illegal weapon he would have plenty to say to him. But he was a good kid.

He looked over. "Are you sure you don't want a soda?"

"No. I'm good. Mom doesn't like me drinking too much of it."

"Right. Good call." Will had been amused earlier that the kid had the same reaction to her pile of wedding stuff on the table as he did. That sparked a conversation topic. "What do you think about her getting married?"

"It's cool."

Will waited for more and when it didn't come, he asked, "So you like Luke?"

"I sort of fixed her up with him. He's the football coach and I'm on the team."

"Don't they both teach at the school?"

"Yeah. But nothing happened until she started picking me up from practice. I hung out in the locker room longer than I needed to and they started talking." He shrugged his thin shoulders. "The rest is history."

"But you like him?"

"He's a pretty cool guy."

"I'm glad to hear it."

Another awkward silence fell. This was not a good time to remember that he'd promised Kim he would have *that* conversation with her son. *Here goes nothing*, he thought.

"You're a pretty good basketball player."

"Thanks. How do you—" Then the light went on. "At the park yesterday."

"Yeah. I saw you in that pick-up game. There were some girls watching. One of them was a cute redhead and she had her eye on you."

Tim didn't look over but his face turned as red as that girl's hair. "Lexie."

"Do you like her?"

"She's okay."

The kid's body language elaborated. There was so much tension he looked ready to snap like a twig.

"I think you like her a lot," Will said. "Have you kissed her?" There was no answer and that was answer enough. "Do you have any questions about anything?"

"Such as?"

"What happens after kissing?"

Tim shook his head. "I know about that."

"What about birth control?" Will figured this would be quicker and easier on both of them if he was more specific. "Condoms."

"What you're saying is that I shouldn't put a girl in the same situation as my mom was with me." His voice was tinged with hostility and a bit of resentment thrown in.

"Yeah. That's what I'm saying." This kid was smart and would know if Will wasn't being completely honest and up front with him. "Just because your mom was young, that doesn't mean she doesn't love you more than anything in the world. I know for a fact she does."

"Yeah. She tells me all the time." He looked over. "And the guy who got her that way ran out on her. And me. He left town and disappeared."

"He did." The rat bastard. But letting his nephew know how ticked off he still was wouldn't help. And he didn't make the same offer he had to his sister to use his detective skills and find him. Will didn't want to put ideas into the kid's head. If he came up with it himself and Kim was on board he would do everything possible to find said rat bastard.

"The thing is, Tim, you and your mom were better off without a guy who would leave like that. And you're lucky. You have family who love you. And that's the most important thing."

"I guess."

"So, if you need condoms…" Will stopped until the boy looked at him. "There are a lot of people for you to turn to. Your mom. But I know that would be weird. Granddad. Luke. Me."

"Okay. Got it."

"Good."

"Can I ask you something, Uncle Will?"

"Sure. Anything." But he braced himself.

"What's the deal with you and April?" Tim glanced over and there was a definite protective expression on his freckled face.

"That's a good question. I wish I knew the answer."

"So you don't know why she turned you down when you asked her out?"

"Nope." Will stuffed the paper their breakfast had been wrapped in back into the bag.

"Well, I like her," the boy said. "And you keep telling everyone that you're only here in town temporarily while Granddad recovers from his surgery. And you said me and my mom are better off without a guy who would walk out on us."

"That's right." It was a good thing he'd braced himself. Will had a feeling he wasn't going to like what came next.

"Maybe if you're not staying you should just leave April alone."

"That would probably be the wisest course of action," Will admitted.

"So, are you going to back off?" Tim asked.

"Can't lie to you, son. I'm not sure."

Because he had a problem. April's rejection made him want to see her even more. Did that make *him* a rat bastard?

After a long day at work, Will walked into Bar None for a beer. It was crowded, apparently the happening place on a summer evening in Blackwater Lake. But, like a heat-seeking missile, his gaze went to a bistro table in the far corner where his sister was having a glass of wine with April. Both women acknowledged him, but April smiled and waved as if she hadn't rejected his dinner invitation a couple nights ago on the Fourth of July. Then she turned her attention back to Kim, clearly shutting him out.

So he headed for the bar and took the only empty stool, which, as luck would have it, afforded an unobstructed view of that corner bistro table where April was pretending she hadn't been acting weird.

Delanie Carlson, the owner of the bar, walked over. The curvy redhead was somewhere in her twenties and had inherited the place from her father. "Hey, Sheriff. How are you?"

"Good." Maybe. He glanced over at April, who was still not looking at him. Forcing a smile, he asked, "You?"

"Oh, you know. Can't complain."

"Looks like business is booming."

"Yeah." Her blue eyes darkened a little as she scanned the place. "What can I get for you?"

"Beer."

"Bottle or tap?"

"Bottle."

"Anything to eat?" When he shook his head, she said, "Okay. One beer coming right up." She walked over to a refrigerator under the bar and pulled out a long-neck bottle. After twisting off the cap, she set it on a napkin in front of him. "Enjoy."

"Thanks." Will didn't want to but couldn't stop himself from looking at April again. If only he could stop dreaming about her, dreams so hot his sheets were practically smoking. He needed a distraction and Delanie was busy.

He glanced at the guy sitting beside him, who was also sipping a beer. Will had never seen him before. "You a tourist?"

"No."

"New in town?"

"Not that new." There was a blank expression on the newcomer's face before he resumed staring at the bottle of beer in front of him.

Will sized him up. He was fit and rugged looking, roughly two hundred pounds with black hair and blue eyes. There was a tattoo on his forearm.

He was starting to get a complex. First April rejected him and now this joker didn't want to talk. It was strictly stubbornness and bad temper that made him pursue this line of questioning. "How long have you been here?"

"More than six months."

"But less than a year," Will guessed. The other guy merely lifted a shoulder. This was starting to feel like an interrogation in that special room with the two-way mirror. "Care to tell me your name?"

"Jack Garner."

"The writer. I read your book."

"Good. I have a mortgage to pay."

"Didn't say I bought it. Just read it."

They stared at each other for several moments and finally Jack said, "Okay. I'll bite. What did you think?"

"It was good." Will was picky about his reading material, but he'd really liked the book. "The action was realistic. I'm guessing you spent some time in the military."

"Army special forces, Ranger division."

That explained why the details were spot-on. "I look forward to the next one."

"Yeah." Jack frowned and took a long pull on his beer.

Will glanced over at April again. She was wearing a pink sweater set with black slacks and had her hair long and silky past her shoulders. She looked so kissable it made him ache. Part of him thought if he stared long enough he'd catch her looking at him. And then what? Even his nephew had advised him to keep his distance. But too often rational thought and hormones didn't see eye to eye. So here he was being pathetic.

"Why don't you just go over there?"

Will met Jack's gaze. "What?"

"You keep staring at that table in the corner. Don't know which one of those ladies you're interested in, but do something about it, man."

"The blonde is my sister and she's engaged."

"Got it." Jack saluted with his beer bottle, letting him know he'd received the warning loud and clear. "So it's the cute brunette."

Jealousy balled in his belly and he wanted to warn him off April, too. But he had no right and that just pissed him off more. "That hasn't been confirmed."

"Yeah, it has. If I were you, I'd just go over there and sit down."

"Who made you my wingman?"

"It's a dirty job, but apparently someone has to do it." Jack looked amused.

"Why would I take your advice?" Will challenged. "Because you know so much about women?"

"What I know about the fairer sex would fit on the head of a pin."

"Then I have to ask: What makes crashing their conversation a good move?"

"It's what you want. You're preoccupied. You're staring at her and it's getting obvious." Jack paused, then added, "And, frankly, you're just not very good company."

Will stared at the other man for a second or two then laughed. "Don't hold back. Tell me how you really feel."

"Will do."

When Jack grinned, Will's gut told him it was something the man rarely did. He held out his hand. "Will Fletcher. Acting sheriff of Blackwater Lake."

"Good to meet you, Sheriff." Jack shook his hand. "Now leave me alone and let me brood."

"Roger that."

Will picked up his beer and headed over to the table where the two women sat. "Mind if I butt in?"

"Hi, Will," his sister said. "Have a seat."

He'd planned to anyway, but it was nice to be invited. "How are you, April?"

"Good, thanks." She gave him a big smile. "So you survived the Fourth of July."

"I did. Here's to that." He held up his beer and they clinked their wineglasses against it.

"I saw you talking to Jack Garner, the writer," his sister said.

"Yeah. Nice guy."

"He doesn't usually talk to anyone when he comes in here," Kim added. "Before you ask how I know that, I should tell you that I don't spend that much time here in the bar. Delanie told me."

"Well he's probably got his reasons for keeping to himself." Will knew some guys on the police force who developed PTSD from incidents related to the job. He figured in army special forces Jack Garner had seen things that changed him, things he didn't want to talk about.

"Actually, Will, I'm glad you're here," his sister said.

That was a surprise. "So I get a pass on crashing girls' night?"

"It's not so much girls' night," April said. "More of an emergency management meeting."

"What's wrong?" He looked from one woman to the other. "You're not calling off the wedding."

"No." Kim's voice was adamant. "But you know all those files and the paperwork on the table the other morning?"

"The crap?" he asked wryly.

"Yeah. That."

"What about it?"

"I'm beginning to be overwhelmed." Kim caught her bottom lip between her teeth.

"You know I was kidding about that, right?" He hadn't meant to freak her out.

"I know. It's just that I'm feeling the pressure. On top of the fact that my dress is back-ordered."

"It just kills me that I can't be your maid of honor," April said.

"I didn't think I needed one. But I also didn't realize there would be this much stuff. Besides, you're my photographer and I know the pictures will be amazing. That's what this is all for. When Luke and I are old we can look at our wedding album and ask who the babies are in the pictures April Kennedy took. It's just the putting-it-all-together part that's getting to me." She sighed. "Maids of honor come and go, but pictures are forever."

Both of the women looked as if they were ready to have an emotional moment that would probably involve tears, and Will was beginning to regret crashing the party. Like most guys, he wanted to fix it. Anything to keep them from crying.

"So pick someone else to be your maid of honor," he suggested. "You have friends, right?"

"Of course I do. But if I ask someone now they'll feel like an afterthought. That might hurt their feelings."

"If they're really your friend, it probably wouldn't be like that," he pointed out.

"Family wouldn't be like that at all," April said. "They would just be there for you because you need them. It's too bad you don't have a sister."

Suddenly there was a gleam in Kim's eyes. "I've got it."

"Unless Dad has a secret baby daughter somewhere, you still don't have one. So what do you have?" Will asked warily.

"A brother and an idea. You can be my maid of honor."

He shook his head. "I don't meet the physical requirements. In case you haven't noticed, I'm not a maid."

"Okay. Man of honor then. Besides, what's in a name? You can be my second, like when duels were fought in the olden days. I think you'd be fantastic, Will."

"He would. What's that police motto? To protect and serve? It takes a guy's guy to be a man of honor." April's voice was pleading.

And Jack Garner was right. She was so cute he wanted her in the worst way. How could he say no to her? "Okay. But if the squad in Chicago finds out about this, I'll get you back," he warned her.

"Oh, Will—" Kim started to cry.

"Oh, for Pete's sake." He handed her a napkin then took her hand in his. "I said yes so you wouldn't cry."

"I'm just happy," she said, dabbing her eyes.

"This calls for a toast," April said. "To Will, the best man of honor you could ask for."

"Probably the only one," he grumbled.

Kim laughed as intended. "To Will."

They touched glasses again and he met April's gaze. She wasn't ignoring him now. She was looking at him as if he'd hung the moon. As if he was her hero.

If he invited her to dinner right this minute would she say yes? Not only did he not want to ask her in front of his sister, a guy's ego could only take so much rejection. Private was better.

He didn't know what April's problem was. Other than the fact that he wasn't staying permanently in Blackwater Lake.

Still, they both knew where the other stood and there wasn't any reason not to have some fun while he was in town. When he got a chance, he planned to pursue that line of questioning.

And he was going to pursue it very soon.

Chapter Seven

April helped Kim carry her wedding dress upstairs. Not only had her first choice arrived without a hitch, it fit like a dream. No alterations required. The bridal shop at Mountain's Edge Mall had offered to store it for her until the wedding, but Kim refused. She'd said everything was starting to feel too out of control and this gave her the illusion of having power over it all.

"I'm guessing this isn't a slip dress." April was wrestling with the bottom half of the heavy, bulky, zippered storage bag.

"Not a chance. I'm a mom, but I've never been married before and this is going to be my dream wedding." There was a note in her voice that hinted at convincing herself more than anyone else.

"Would it be this heavy in a dream?" April asked, trying to tease her friend's nerves into submission. It was obvious that asking Will to be her man of honor hadn't taken the edge off the pressure she was feeling. "How are you going to move in this dress?"

"On my day I will float on air," Kim assured her.

They finally made it upstairs and turned left toward Kim's room. Her son's, which his mother often said could be mistaken for a biohazard waste dump, was right next door. April knew Will slept across the hall.

She forced herself not to look in that direction and check out where he was hanging his hat these days. He hadn't asked her out again, but the other night at Bar None he'd joined her and Kim. He seemed to have a good time and April did, too. It felt a little like a date and she hoped Kim's strategy of making Will work for it wouldn't cost her a chance to go out with him.

"I guess Will isn't home yet."

"If he was, I'd have made him haul this behemoth up the stairs." Kim backed into her room, pushing open the door with her shoulder. "It's the least the man of honor can do."

"It was really sweet of him to agree to do that."

"I know, right?" Kim waited for April to bring the bottom half of the bag into the room. Instead of sliding doors, her walk-in closet had a closing one with a metal hook on the outside. They managed to put the dress's heavy-duty hanger on it. She looked at April and blew out a breath. "It just felt appropriate to ask Will to stand up with me. If it can't be you."

"Could have knocked me over with a feather when those words came out of your mouth," April admitted. "I thought you were kidding."

"I was a little. At first. Then I realized I could really use someone. I'm not even sure what for because you've been there for me, for everything."

April's gaze drifted to the zippered garment bag. "Can we look at it again?"

"Twist my arm." Kim reached up and unzipped the bag, letting the full tulle skirt spill out.

They stared at the strapless bodice, sparkling with crystals and tapering to a fitted waist, where the full skirt flared out. It oozed femininity.

April sighed. "I can just picture it all. The roses and lilies, with a few hydrangeas thrown in for color in your bride's bouquet. Hank, Tim and Will in their black tuxes. Guests gathered for the happy occasion."

"Yeah." Kim's voice was a little shaky.

Time for a pep talk. "Then you walk down the aisle, where the man of your dreams is waiting next to the minister who will preside over your vows."

"That's the plan."

"Are you writing them?" April asked. Her friend was most confident with the written word and loved instructing her students in the art of essay writing. "If Blackwater Lake High School's favorite English teacher doesn't write her own vows, what kind of message would that send?"

"Not a good one, I'm guessing." Doubt crept into her expression.

"Oh," April said staring at the stunningly beautiful dress. "You're going to look so gorgeous in this when you become Mrs. Luke Miller."

"Oh, God—" Kim's eyes widened.

April thought maybe this was a good time to take the focus off the dress. She spotted several boxes in the corner and walked over to peek inside. "The invitations. They're beautiful." She picked one up and ran a hand over the embossed white lily and read the words out loud. "Mr. Henry Fletcher and Mr. and Mrs. Frank Miller request the honor of your presence at the wedding of their children, Miss Kimberly Fletcher and Mr. Luke Miller."

"Do you really like them?"

April had helped her pick them out. "Even better than I thought. These came out so great. It's going to be official."

"Eek—"

There was a knock on the open bedroom door. "Anyone home?"

"Will, I didn't hear you come in." Kim looked at her wristwatch. "It's late."

"Long day. Some tourists having a little too much fun." His gaze was on April when he said the last word. There was a smoky look in his eyes and a rough edge to his voice that hinted at the kind of fun a man and woman needed privacy for.

Or maybe that was just her imagination, April thought, because she'd had that kind of fun on her mind since this dating-and-dumping plan had started.

"Hi, Will," she said.

He nodded, then looked at the dress and whistled. "I guess you got the one you wanted."

"Uh-huh." Kim bit her lip uncertainly.

"And you rode shotgun," he said to April.

"Yeah." Her gaze was on her friend, who'd turned a little pale.

"I'm kind of new at this man-of-honor thing. Is it in my job description to stand guard now over this big, poofy ball of white?"

Apparently those words pushed Kim over the edge because she burst into tears.

"I was kidding." Will looked at April and said, "What did I say?"

"N-nothing. It's me," Kim blubbered.

"What's wrong with you?"

"Everything," she wailed.

"Like I said, I've got no experience with this MOH stuff, but I'm a quick learner." He took his sister's hand, led her over to the bed and sat her on the floral spread before going down on one knee in front of her. "It would help me out a lot if you'd be a little more specific about what the problem is."

"I think I'm making a big mistake." She buried her face in her hands and sobbed.

Will met April's gaze with a look that said he would rather do police paperwork in triplicate than deal with a weeping woman. He stared at the floor for several moments, shaking his head. Any second she expected him to bail. Say something about a hysterical woman being above his pay grade. Or advise his sister to walk it off.

Finally he sighed, then said, "Kimmie—"

"W-what?"

He stood, then sat on the bed beside her and settled his strong arm around her shoulders. "Why do you think getting married is a mistake?"

"It just is."

"So you don't love Luke?"

"Of course I love him." She lowered her hands and stared at her brother as if he were crazy. "He's handsome, funny, kind and loving. Sexy."

"Too much information," Will said.

"The point is that Luke is everything I've ever wanted in a man."

"Okay. Then your son doesn't like him?"

"Tim likes Luke a lot. He played matchmaker for us."

"Okay." One corner of Will's mouth curved up. "He actually told me that when we went fishing. So, moving on. Obviously his parents think you're not good enough for their son."

"Don't be ridiculous." She sniffled. "His family likes me better than him. And they love Tim. Already they're insisting he call them Grandma and Grandpa."

"Okay. Then there's something here that I'm not see-ing," he said.

Brilliant strategy, April thought. Will was going through everything step-by-step to eliminate her fears instead of just telling her it would be okay.

"Maybe Luke and I should just go to Vegas," Kim said.

"So it's the big, showy wedding that's freaking you out," he deduced.

"Some," she admitted, meeting his gaze. "There are a lot of details to take care of. What if I forget something? Worse, what if it's all a huge mistake, and Luke and I end up hating each other?"

"That's not going to happen." Will was adamant.

"How can you be so sure?"

"Because you've kissed a lot of frogs and waited for the right guy." He lifted her hand and put it in his big palm, then folded his fingers around hers. "Take it from some-one who didn't wait and got it wrong."

His gaze settled on April when he said the last words. Her legs wobbled and she locked her knees to keep from toppling over. His blue eyes darkened to the color of the lake and more than anything she wanted to drown in them.

"I never liked the woman you married," Kim said.

"Yeah." He smiled at her declaration. "You've made that abundantly clear. More than once."

"Sorry."

"Does Luke know you're the queen of saying I told you so?"

"You'd have to ask him." But she laughed for the first time. "I guess it's just everything getting to me. The in-vitations. The dress. Food and flowers. Writing vows. It's getting real. And pretty darn scary."

"A normal reaction," he reassured her.

"Yeah?"

"No question. Anyone who doesn't have a meltdown and take inventory of the situation shouldn't be doing it."

"I guess you passed the test," April said.

"Tests are good," Kim agreed.

"So says the teacher." Will pulled her in for a bear hug. "You waited for the right guy and deserve to have a big party to celebrate. It's going to be perfect."

Kim nodded. "You're right. Thanks for talking me off the ledge."

"What's a man of honor for?"

His sister smiled and nodded, then said, "I need to go wash my face."

"I was going to say," he teased. "You look a little puffy."

She laughed, then left the room.

April released a breath. "It happened so fast. I was excited about the dress and the wedding and couldn't stop talking. When I realized she was starting to panic it was too late."

"Bound to happen," he said.

"You were amazing with her." His gentle common sense, reassurance and understanding tugged at April's heart. "You even used your own experience to convince her she was making the right choice."

"That's me. A horrible warning." But there was laughter in his eyes when he said the words.

"I didn't mean it like that. You did really good today, Will Fletcher."

And as gooey as she was feeling inside, it was probably just as well she hadn't gone out with him. This was a sweet side of Will, the side that could break her heart again if she wasn't careful.

Just because he admitted that he got it wrong with April before didn't mean the two of them could get it right now.

* * *

April put a low-cal, frozen chicken-enchilada dinner in her microwave to cook and tried to convince herself she wasn't lonely, bordering on pathetic. She had a successful business and loved her work. Lots of people called her friend. But all were married with the exception of Kim, whose single status would change about six weeks from now before summer ended.

The truth was that Kim's approaching marriage hadn't made her think this way; the engagement had happened months ago. These feelings hadn't surfaced until Will came back to town. Along with him came old memories that she'd managed to put away. Memories of runs, dinners, movie dates. Memories of not being by herself.

She was over him. Really. But it had been more than a week since he'd asked her out and she'd turned him down. Kim's reasoning seemed sort of lame now, all things considered. Only three days ago he'd reasoned his sister out of a meltdown. Then April and Will had had a moment alone in Kim's bedroom, which she was certain had been a *moment*. After that…nothing.

"They don't call. They don't write," she muttered, listening to the hum of the microwave. And for real excitement she watched her frozen dinner turning inside the appliance.

Then things got exciting. At the same time the microwave beeped a signal that her cheese enchiladas were now warm and probably rubbery, there was a knock on her kitchen door. That made it official. She might be lonely, but pathetic was off the table because someone wanted to see her.

"Please let it not be a door-to-door salesman," she pleaded.

Although they'd ring the bell beside the front door. It

was probably one of the Fletchers—Hank, Kim, Tim or Will. Her money was on the first three.

After turning on the outside light, she saw Will through the sliding glass door and knew she'd have lost her bet. Her heart started thumping. Hard. But that was only because she was so happy to see *someone*. Anyone. And he had something in his hands that looked suspiciously like a pizza. There weren't many things that could fit in a big square flat box.

April unlocked the door and slid it open. "Hi."

"I come bearing food. And wine." There was a bottle of red tucked under his arm. It was starting to rain and the outside light made drops of moisture sparkle in his dark hair. "In the spirit of full disclosure, I have to tell you it's a bribe."

"Oh?" She stepped back to let him in out of the rain, then closed the door behind him.

"I need asylum."

"Did you say *an* asylum?" she teased.

"If you don't let me in, that's exactly where I'll be headed." He almost looked dead serious, but there was a hint of laughter in his eyes.

It was surprising how well she still knew him, could still read him. "What's wrong?"

"Nothing, I guess. As far as I can tell, there's not a crisis but Kim is making everything wedding into a federal case. It's driving me nuts." He set the pizza box and wine on the island and looked at her.

April remembered the pleading expression from a lifetime ago. It was the one that could get her to do anything. Of course that was a time when it took very little to get her to do whatever he wanted because she'd been blinded by love.

"So, what do you want? Define asylum."

"As God is my witness, I will be the world's best man of honor my sister ever had, but I can only do that if I can recharge my batteries with someone normal and reasonable."

"Where's Kim now?"

"Out with Luke."

"So, last time I checked your dad and nephew were normal and rational."

"They're not home."

So he'd been alone. Did that mean he was lonely, too? Just moments ago she'd been feeling sorry for herself and now those feelings transferred to him.

"Okay." She nodded. "I'll throw together a salad. You open the wine."

"Roger that." He saluted, then frowned at the intermittent noise coming from the microwave. "What's that sound?"

"My frozen dinner."

He made a face and managed to look adorable. "So a case could be made for me rescuing you from a tasteless, plastic meal."

"One could say that, but one would be wrong." She pulled the small, pathetic, individual dinner out of the microwave to stop the annoying sound and dropped it in the trash. "This particular entrée is one of my favorites."

"That's obvious by the way you couldn't get rid of it fast enough."

"Okay." She couldn't stop a smile. "You're the one who set a high bar for full disclosure. Pizza is so much better than what I was going to have. You did rescue me." She gave him an adoring look and batted her lashes. "My hero."

"Aw shucks, ma'am." He picked up the bottle of wine and asked, "Where's your corkscrew?"

"That cylindrical red thing on the counter to the left of the oven."

He walked over and picked it up. "You have an electric one?"

"It's an investment."

"In what?"

"Independence. Women's liberation. Whatever you want to call it. I just needed to know I could get a cork out of a wine bottle without a man around to pull it out with brute strength."

Was that a flirty remark? It felt a little flirty, but lately she'd been pretending with him. And it had been so long since she'd done it with any man, her flirt-meter was rusty. But she was pretty sure she'd just nailed him with genuine, authentic flirtation material.

The thing was, no effort had been involved and that was due in no small part to her attraction, which was completely natural and extremely powerful. The challenge wasn't in flirting with him, but in not letting it be more.

"Okay," he said. "Since I've got nothing to prove regarding my masculinity, I'm okay using the girly opener."

"Good thing. It's the only one I've got. Your other choice would be to get the cork out by hitting the bottle on the edge of the granite and whacking off the top."

He laughed and the sound brought back more memories that grabbed at her heart. When they were together, talking had always turned to teasing and that turned sexy, which led to making love. Since that was her endgame, his need for sanctuary worked to her advantage. But somehow the whole thing felt dishonest.

"Something wrong, April?"

His voice snapped her out of the conscience attack. "No. I'll get the salad made."

She turned the oven on low and put the pizza in to keep it warm while getting everything else ready. In ten minutes they were sitting across from each other at the square oak table in the kitchen nook with a meal in front of them. Slices of pizza on paper plates. Salad in bright orange pottery bowls. Stemless glasses containing a deep maroon–colored wine.

Will held up his glass. "To—" He thought for a moment, then shrugged and said, "I've got nothing."

"How about to friends who are willing to take you in as long as you bring the pizza and wine?"

"I like it." He touched his glass to hers, then took a sip.

April did the same, set her glass down before digging into the pizza. It was like a party in her mouth, as she savored the blended flavors of cheese, tomato sauce, sausage and black olives. With her mouth full, she said, "This is my favorite."

"I know. You think I'd have begged you to take me in with anything less than your beloved first choice?"

"I'm just surprised. I didn't think you'd remember."

"Then prepare to be surprised again." He thought for a moment. "I remember that you don't like ketchup on your fries because it camouflages the exquisite taste of a perfectly good potato. Same goes for flavored chips. You're a traditional-chip girl who doesn't like it messed up."

"Hmm." This was a little disconcerting. Nice. Flattering, but unsettling.

"I also remember no ground pepper on your salad. You like guacamole but a naked avocado makes you gag. Toast or English muffin has to be well done and you credit, or blame, your mother for that. When she got distracted, anything in the toaster burned, but money for a single mom raising a daughter was tight. No food in your house got wasted, so she somehow convinced you the black part was good for you. And now you have to have it that way."

April somehow managed to keep tears from welling in her eyes. It wasn't easy, what with him talking about the mother she still missed terribly. On top of that she was moved that he recalled the silly little things she'd shared with him.

"Wow. Your powers of recall are impressive." And touching. "Okay. Two can play this game."

"This is a game?" One dark eyebrow rose questioningly.

"It's called reminiscing." She tapped her lip, searching through the amazing stack of recollections. "I remember that you like a steak so rare it's practically mooing on the plate. You prefer rice to potatoes, but mac and cheese is the carbohydrate gold standard. And raw spinach in a salad is acceptable, but cooked is slimy."

He finished chewing a bite of pizza. "Gold star for you, missy."

"Thank you very much." She drank some wine, nearly finishing what was in the glass.

Will picked up the bottle and refilled them both. "You cry at sad movies and jump out of your skin at scary ones."

"Busted." She smiled, thinking about how she used to hide her face against his shoulder when they saw a horror flick. These days she just didn't go to that genre. "And you preferred science and discovery channels on TV as opposed to scripted comedies and dramas."

"Still do." He looked at her, something dark and intense in his eyes. "It's nice to know some things don't change."

"Yeah." She drank some wine, a wistful, reflective feeling settling over her.

They finished the meal in relative silence, each of them thinking their own thoughts. Doing the dishes together was another thing that hadn't changed. There weren't many from this meal, but on the rare occasions she'd cooked for him and the two of them were alone, he'd always insisted on helping to clean up. It was the least he could do since she'd done the hard part.

She closed the dishwasher door and finished the wine in her glass. Since the bottle was now empty that meant she was responsible for half of it disappearing and the buzz she was rocking didn't come as a surprise. It was also liberating, as in the censor between her brain and her mouth was buzzed, too. That meant it wasn't functioning efficiently to filter her thoughts.

All this talking about the past brought up good memories but also bad. April hadn't forgotten that he'd cast her aside for another woman. There was a question she'd never had a chance to ask, but she did now thanks to two glasses of wine.

"Why did your marriage break up, Will?"

Chapter Eight

Because she wasn't you.

The thought popped into Will's mind and he was a little stunned. But maybe he shouldn't be. The other day while his sister was freaking out he'd told her she waited until Luke came along and got it right. He hadn't waited and got it wrong because the woman he'd proposed to wasn't April. He hadn't said as much to Kim, but it must have been in the back of his mind.

He would probably regret that decision for the rest of his life.

And now he was lucky enough to be standing in her kitchen after sharing pizza and a bottle of wine. It was more than he deserved.

"Will?" April held up her hands. "Never mind. Forget I said anything. I shouldn't have asked. It's really none of my business and, for the record, I'm blaming it on the wine. Seriously, I'm sorry—"

He touched a finger to her lips to stop the words. "You have nothing to apologize for. I don't mind telling you what happened. More than anyone else you have a right to know. Obviously, you already realize what an idiot I am."

"I don't think it's fair or right to factor in IQ in terms of relationship analysis. Being smart has nothing to do with matters of the heart." She leaned back against the counter in front of the sink and folded her arms over her chest. "For what it's worth, I don't think you're an idiot."

He stood across from her with the kitchen island to his back. "You're very gracious even though I don't deserve it."

"No, you don't," she teased. "But I can't help it. A flaw in my personality."

"Okay. As flaws go it's not bad." He smiled, then wondered how it was that she could do that when he was contemplating this deeply personal disappointment in himself. It was a mistake he still took very hard. Maybe telling her would be a good thing, help put it to rest forever. "The reality is that the marriage was doomed from the start."

"Why do you say that?"

Will didn't expect to hear genuine sympathy in her voice. Probably because he'd treated her so badly and felt fortunate that she was even talking to him. She had every right to be glad things hadn't worked out for him. Who could blame her for it? But he didn't see anything like that in the compassionate expression on her face.

"She was just there, a bar where cops hang out after a shift. She was pretty. Flirty."

"That's not good."

For the life of him he couldn't figure out why she looked guilty all of a sudden. Maybe she did have a little he-got-what-was-coming-to-him going on.

"Anyway, she was there and available. I was lonely."

"I understand." A little sadness crept into her voice.

Now it was his turn to feel guilty. He looked down at her and in the dim light he could see sorrow on her face, a bruised expression in her eyes for just a moment. Because he'd been the one who moved to Chicago and left behind everything and everyone he'd known, he thought loneliness was exclusive to him. Now he saw how selfish that was. He realized April must have been lonely, too, and she'd stayed behind in the town where they'd fallen in love. That must have been a different kind of loneliness.

Alone in a crowd.

"It's no excuse for what I did to you, but it is the truth."

"I really do understand, Will."

He studied her expression, then nodded. "Anyway, I proposed to her and she said yes. There was no cooling-off period. We went to city hall and got married. It was all downhill from there."

"What happened?" She crossed one foot over the other at the ankles.

"I wanted to make detective, so when anyone asked me for anything, any extra work, I was the go-to guy. Special task force on drugs. Working with vice. Stakeouts for illegal weapons trafficking. You name it, I did it."

"Didn't she understand that you were trying to move up in the department?"

"I told her that. More than once."

Will remembered the endless arguments about him not being around. The accusations that everything and everyone was more important than her. His response was standard-issue—he was there now and she'd picked a fight.

"We had some pretty loud discussions," he said.

"Did you try marriage counseling?"

"I suggested it and she came back with something sarcastic like I was never home as it was. I couldn't fit her in, so how could I manage to see a shrink?"

"I hate to say this, Will, but that's a valid point given what you just told me."

One of the things he liked about her was that reasonable streak and he couldn't fault her for it now.

"Yeah." He dragged his fingers through his hair. "I know. And I was about to concede that point to her when she accused me of using work to avoid her."

"Was she right?"

"At the time I was defensive, but now that I have some distance it's fair to say there was some truth to her accusation."

"But nothing changed." April wasn't asking a question.

He'd made an effort to be around more. Turned down some extra assignments. "How can you know that?"

"Because you're not married to her anymore." She shrugged as if that explained it all. And she was right.

"No, we're not married." Duh. And whatever pathetic attempt he'd made hadn't changed the inevitable split. "I approached her about a trial separation, to see if we'd be happier apart. And it took me a while to bring it up. I didn't want to hurt her."

"What did she say?"

"She bypassed the idea of separating and went straight for divorce. Said there was no point in dragging things out longer than necessary."

"How did you feel about that?"

"You sound like a shrink," he commented.

She lifted one shoulder. "When I take portrait photographs, I ask a lot of questions. That brings out emotions that the camera captures. It's a habit."

"I'll remember that. And the truth is that when she wanted to end things permanently I was relieved."

"Obviously that was the right decision, then."

"It feels wrong," he said.

"Why?"

"I always wanted what my parents had before my mom died in the car accident. They were crazy about each other. Held hands and kissed in public. Kim and I used to give them a hard time about embarrassing us, but they didn't care."

"I remember." She smiled fondly at the memory.

"And Kim always said she was the family screwup, getting pregnant at seventeen. The thing is she never made the mistake of marrying the jerk. She waited until she knew it was right."

"Everyone's journey is different, Will," April said reasonably. "No one gets out of this life without regrets of one kind or another."

"I know," he said. "But being the family failure is hard for me."

"Because you've always been the guy in the white hat, righting wrongs and fighting the good fight."

"Truth, justice and the American way. Superman, that's me. But I messed up."

"That's one way of looking at it. Or one could make an argument that you saw things weren't working out and did the right thing for both of you." She straightened away from the counter. "But here's something your father always says. It's not our successes that reveal character. It's how we handle our mistakes that defines us. Your actions don't sound like a failure to me."

"You're cutting me slack I don't deserve."

"Oh, Will—" She hesitated a moment, then took two steps toward him and moved in close, wrapping her arms around his waist. "It really is way past time to stop beating yourself up about what happened in the past."

Will was having a hard time processing her words, what with that sweet little body pressed to his. He could feel her small firm breasts and her soft cheek resting against his chest. The scent of flowers drifted to him from her hair and he couldn't stop himself from wrapping her in his arms.

"April—" There was a hitch in his voice as a powerful yearning ground through him.

When she raised her head and looked up at him, he kissed her. Their lips met for one beat, then two. In the next second they couldn't get enough of each other. She met him more than halfway and above the swishing of the dishwasher he could hear the sound of their heavy breathing and her soft moans that made him hot as a firecracker.

"I never thought I would get a chance to kiss you again," Will said in a husky, edgy whisper against her lips.

The words sent a crushing cascade of guilt down on April that was as effective as a bucket of cold water in destroying the mood. More than anything she wanted to go where this kiss was leading, but she just couldn't do it. She couldn't get past the fact that this was part of a pre-meditated plan to flirt, fall into bed, then dump him in the name of closure.

Now the plan felt all kinds of wrong.

She stepped out of Will's arms. "I can't do this."

"I'm sorry? What?" He stared at her.

"I can't do it."

"What exactly?" Surprise and frustration merged in his voice.

"Kiss you." She hesitated. "And whatever else might follow after that. I just can't. Not like this."

"Well…" He blew out a long breath. "Just the Cliff's Notes of biology here, but *this* is pretty much the only way to do it."

"No." She twisted her fingers together. "You don't understand."

"You're right. I don't. And, honey, at this moment I don't really want to." There was a lot of lust in the look he settled on her.

"And I don't really want to tell you. But, like I said before, you set a high bar for full disclosure. So whether you want to or not, you have to hear this."

"Okay, then. If I agree to listen, can we pick up where we just left off?"

"Trust me. You're not going to want to do that." When he found out she was a scheming, underhanded, devious witch, he wouldn't want anything to do with her.

"Let me be the judge of that. Because right now I want to kiss you more than anything. And unless you tell me you're a man, which I know for a fact isn't true, there's not much you could say to change my mind." His blue eyes turned darker and focused a lot of intensity on her mouth.

It was so tempting to say "Gotcha" or "Just kidding" and continue kissing him, but she realized the weight of this secret was crushing.

"Okay. Here goes." April stood up straighter and met his gaze. "I'm kissing you under false pretenses."

"I'm not sure what that means." He tilted his head, studying her. "Are you saying you didn't like it?"

"No," she said adamantly.

"Because it sure felt to me as if you were really into it."

"I really was," she assured him.

"Good. No offense, but I don't think you're that good an actress." The corners of his mouth curved up. "I'm a detective. I know when someone's trying to pull a fast one and that's not what you were doing. Trust me on this, you couldn't lie your way out of a paper bag."

"Thanks, I think."

"So, define false pretenses."

"Okay." She twisted her fingers together, trying to figure out how to word this confession. "After you came to see me when you first got back to Blackwater Lake, I had a heart-to-heart talk with Kim."

"I knew she was somehow involved. You two are as thick as thieves."

Kind of an appropriate analogy, but he really had no idea, she thought. "Don't blame Kim."

"I can't blame anyone until you tell me what's going on."

"Right." She didn't want to tell him the whole truth, about how hard it had been seeing him again, the painful feelings he'd stirred up. "Kim and I got to talking. This is a small town and people have a way of knowing everything that goes on. And they have long memories. I realized that since you and I broke up, I've always been the poor girl that Will Fletcher left behind. Your sister was just thinking out loud and remarked that I never got closure from our relationship. It all went down on your terms."

"That's true." He nodded and the shadows in his eyes said he regretted what happened. "I'm sorry, April—"

She held up her hand. "Please don't say that. The thing is that Kim had an idea for how I could get closure." She stopped because as soon as she told him the rest of it, he was going to leave and never speak to her again. April couldn't really blame him, but, wow, this was really so much harder than she'd expected.

"What was her idea?" Oddly, Will didn't look wary or angry. Not even a little upset. More amused than anything else.

She blew out a long breath, then forced herself to meet his gaze. "The plan was for me to flirt with you. Have a fling. Then be the one to end it so everyone in Blackwater Lake would stop pitying me."

"So that's why you looked guilty when I mentioned my ex-wife was flirty when we met."

"Yes." April was surprised he'd noticed, then realized she shouldn't be. He *was* a detective—a good one—and trained to pay attention to reactions. It was probably impossible for him to turn off his powers of observation. "And look how that turned out."

"I knew something was up with you," he said.

"No way." Surely she hadn't been that obvious. "I don't believe it."

"After that first meeting in your shop when we talked, every time I saw you, you acted funny. Did something weird with your eyes. Now I realize that was you flirting. Or trying to." He looked awfully smug. "I guess I should be relieved that you're not very good at it."

That didn't sound like an angry, resentful man who was going to set a speed record for walking out. But it could be payback for her scheming him. Or trying to. "Why relieved?"

"Because eventually you forgot to pretend and behaved naturally. When you flirted, and you did, it obviously was sincere."

She narrowed her gaze at him. "Look, Will, don't be nice to me. I don't deserve it. Just leave. I know you want to. We'll call it closure and move on."

"Who says I want to leave?"

Now she was really confused. "I was dishonest with you. Why would you want to stay?"

There was a smokin' hot look in his eyes when he said, "Because I really want to take you to bed."

"Oh, my—" April's heart started beating so fast she couldn't seem to form words. That required a thought process coming from a brain that wasn't fried. Finally she managed to say, "I don't see how it's possible that you would want me after what I just told you."

"I understand," he said simply. "I get how this town works and what you've been going through. On top of that, you get points for coming clean." He moved closer, until their bodies were barely touching.

"But the fact that I could even do that—" She caught her top lip between her teeth.

"The thing is, you didn't really do it. There's evidence that my sister has been, shall we say involved, since the beginning." There was the steely-eyed detective. "Do you have an on-again, off-again thing with a ski instructor named Jean Luc?"

"No." But she couldn't help smiling.

"My sister has always been good at making stuff up." He nodded. "And when I asked you out— There's a reason you said no, isn't there?"

She sighed. "I hate to rat out your sister, but she convinced me that playing hard to get was the best way to get a man to notice you."

"Not in your case. All you have to do is walk into a room." His voice went all husky and deep. "So, my sister has been more invested in this mission than you are probably aware."

"Please don't be mad at her."

"I'm not." And he truly didn't look peeved. "But it shows how much you need to convince this town that you're here because you want to be and not because you were left behind."

"That's true." Pretty much.

He stared at her for several moments. "So, I have an idea."

"Your sister had one, too. Apparently it's in the Fletcher DNA." She blew out a breath. "I'm afraid to ask what it is."

"You don't have to ask. I'm happy to share." He reached out and tucked her hair behind her ear. "If you want a fling, I'm completely open to that."

"Wow, you're such a giver." Her pulse was going wild at the suggestion. But rational thought managed to break free of the sensual haze. "There's just one problem with your idea."

"And that is?"

"At the end of the summer you're leaving Blackwater Lake. I'll still be the girl you left behind. Twice."

"I see your point." He nodded thoughtfully. "Okay. How about this? We have a fling and before I leave, you can publicly dump me."

"Where's public?" she asked skeptically.

"You pick the place."

"Main Street? Farmer's market on Sunday morning? The Grizzly Bear Diner?"

"Any or all of the above," he agreed.

She thought it over and deemed the terms to be very generous. Besides, she really wanted him and the yearning inside her was turning into an unbearable ache. She held out her hand. "You've got yourself a deal."

He took her fingers into his large palm and squeezed, then released her and scooped her into his arms. When she wrapped her arms around his neck, he nuzzled her cheek and whispered into her ear, "I've got something else in mind to seal this deal."

His breath on her ear sent tingles skittering through her body. They'd been heading in this direction ever since she'd brought him that chicken casserole and he'd invited her in for a glass of wine.

He carried her as if she weighed nothing and she knew

that wasn't true. But the gesture made her feel safe, protected, not alone. And, being completely honest, it was romantic. He swept her away, literally, into her bedroom. As long as she didn't get swept away for real, where was the harm? She was no longer that young girl who was barely a woman. She was fully grown with a mind of her own and knew what she wanted.

And she wanted Will.

He set her on her feet beside the bed and cupped her cheek in one hand as he lowered his mouth to hers. The fire she'd banked in order to get her confession out burst into flame once again. They kissed and kissed, trying desperately to get closer, but it wasn't enough. He was a great kisser and she could do it forever, preferably without clothes.

In the next moment, as if he could read her mind, he was pushing at her shirt, yanking it up over her head. Before it hit the floor, she was shoving at his T-shirt and he pulled it free and threw the thing somewhere. Shoes were kicked off and the rest of their clothes were tossed anywhere. Will reached around her and hauled the quilted bedspread down to the foot along with the blanket and sheet.

Then his hard-muscled body and heat were pressed up against her, nudging her toward the mattress. She sat and scooted over to make room for him, but before joining her he reached for his jeans and took something from his wallet.

Condom. Thank you, God.

He slid in beside her and gathered her close, letting their bodies come together, bare skin to bare skin. The feeling was indescribable and the dusting of hair on his chest tickled her breasts in the most erotic possible way. She leaned back far enough and brushed a hand over the contour of muscle and grazed his nipple with her thumb, causing him to hiss out a breath.

"Problem?" she teased.

"Not unless you stop." His voice was ragged.

So she did it again and he groaned before nudging her to her back. He kissed her neck, then moved lower and sucked the tip of her breast into his mouth. With his tongue he flicked the nipple, then pulled back to blow softly on the wetness. It drove her wild and she'd forgotten how much she loved him doing that. She couldn't believe he'd remembered. And that wasn't all.

He kissed and nipped his way down her body until she was writhing with need.

"Will, I don't think I can wait—" She could hardly breathe. "Please…"

"Your wish—" His voice was so low it was barely audible.

He reached over to the nightstand and grabbed the packet, then ripped it open. After rolling it on, he came back to her and settled himself between her legs.

Slowly he filled her and the sensation simultaneously stole her breath and made her sigh. He moved inside her, a measured rhythm meant to retrace steps from their last time together.

But April wanted more. She wanted now. And she wanted new.

Her hands wandered over his body, tracing lightly over his abdomen until he groaned. He lowered his body closer to hers, limiting her wandering hands. She smiled, knowing he didn't want to be rushed but doing it anyway. Lifting her head, she drew close enough to kiss his neck, tracing his earlobe with her tongue.

"April—"

"I know."

And then she lost track of everything, preoccupied with her senses, just letting her body feel and build slowly, breathing faster and faster. Without much warning she went right over the edge and cried out as pleasure rolled like a thunderstorm through her. He held her close and pressed deeper, then deeper still until he groaned and followed her over that sensuous cliff. They clung to each other until their breathing returned almost to normal.

Will exhaled slowly then kissed her forehead before rolling out of bed. "I'll be right back. Don't you dare go anywhere."

As if, she thought.

She didn't think she could have moved if her life depended on it. Her body was happy and relaxed. She closed her eyes, but was aware when the light in the bathroom went on. A minute later the room was in shadow again and Will was back.

He slid into bed, pulled the sheet up over them then drew her to his side with one strong arm holding her close to him.

"And that's how you really seal a deal."

"I like it," she said drowsily.

She was too sleepy and sated to realize all the implications of sex with Will. Her only thought before falling asleep was how very much she liked this fling thing.

Chapter Nine

April closing up shop for the day April drove home, parked her compact car in the driveway, then walked straight across the alley to the Fletchers' back door. Kim had called and said they needed to talk, so here she was, knocking on the door.

Almost instantly her friend answered and grinned. "So, my brother sneaked out of your house late last night. Or was it early this morning?"

"More like late last night," April confirmed.

She smiled and felt as if she'd been doing that all day. Surely everyone she'd seen had known that she had sex with Will Fletcher last night and didn't regret it.

"Is it safe to assume that the two of you didn't spend all those hours discussing old times?"

"It is safe to assume that." April sighed. "There was physical activity involved."

"You slept with Will." Kim looked both pleased and aggravated. "He's never even taken you out to dinner."

April followed her into the Fletchers' kitchen. "Keep your voice down. It's possible they didn't hear you in Cleveland and I'd like to keep it that way."

The two of them stood by the island. "Dad and Tim are out and Will isn't home from work yet."

"Seriously, Kim, he actually has taken me out to dinner."

"Not since you set out to seduce him."

Wow, April hadn't really done that, at least not by herself. If seduction had been involved, both of them were guilty. A little pizza. A little wine… Will kissed her and they both went up in flames.

"To put a finer point on it," she said, "He did buy dinner. He brought over a pizza because the wedding stuff was getting to him and he needed a calm place to decompress."

"Oh, please. He's not that delicate. And, just so we're clear, that's not the same as going out and doesn't count." Then Kim tsked before grinning broadly. "Was it awesome?"

April felt heat creep into her cheeks when she thought about the way he'd touched her. Everywhere. And she'd been like putty in his hands. "Yes."

"And?"

"I'm not sure there's anything more to add."

"Where do things stand between you? Where do you go from here? What are your expectations?"

"We're just going to have fun." Then April decided her friend should know the whole truth. "Don't be mad, but—"

"That's never a good way to start a sentence."

"I told him about the plan to dump him. And that it was your idea. For the record he guessed that you were involved. I'm sorry." She studied her friend's expression, trying to gauge her level of annoyance. "I just couldn't go to bed with him and not tell him about the plan."

"I knew you couldn't do it." Kim smiled. "You're so honest and it's why I love you. But I knew if things headed in that direction you'd never seal the deal without spilling the beans."

"So you're not mad?"

"Did you have a good time?" the other woman asked.

"Yes." April felt the glow from deep in her soul and wondered why Kim even had to ask.

"Then no way I could be mad. You haven't looked this happy in a very long time and it's wonderful to see." She turned serious. "Are you okay with this just being a summer thing?"

"I know he's leaving when Hank goes back to work. This time I'm going into it with my eyes open. So, yeah, I'm okay with it." She snapped her fingers. "I forgot the best part. He agreed to let me publicly dump him before he leaves."

"He's a good man," Kim said fondly.

The front door opened and closed. Moments later the man in question walked into the kitchen. He smiled at April. "Hi."

"How was your day?" She smiled back, fully aware that the glow she'd been rocking all day had just amped up by a factor of a hundred.

"Good."

"Don't mind me," Kim said. "Just pretend I'm not here." Will looked at her. "Hi."

"Hey." She looked from him to April. "Luke is picking me up in a few minutes. We're going to Bar None for a drink and dinner. You guys should come with us. We'll make it a double date."

"And why would we want to do that?" Will asked.

"Because you owe her a dinner after what you did last night."

April looked at him and shrugged. "She saw you coming out of my house at an indecent hour."

"Who put you on sibling surveillance?" It was hard to tell whether or not he was annoyed at getting caught.

"I made her tell me what happened," Kim confirmed. "And, just so you know, I approve."

"I'd expect nothing less." Will's expression was wry. "After all, it was your idea."

"You don't have to thank me." His sister waved a hand dismissively. "Just say you agree to a double date. You and April. Luke and me. It will be fun. We've never done that before."

"So why should we do it now?" he said and sent April a look that said he was deliberately giving her a hard time.

"If you don't," she warned, "I'll tell Dad you spent the night at April's."

"I'm willing to take my chances." The look on his face was one that he reserved for torturing his sister. "On second thought we should go with her and Luke."

"I'll bite," April said. "Why?"

"I haven't had a chance to really get acquainted with the man my sister is going to marry. Maybe he should know what she's really like."

"Do your worst," Kim challenged. "You don't scare me."

"What do you say, April? Are you up for a double date?" he asked.

She had the ridiculous feeling that she would follow him anywhere. And this wasn't the first time she'd experienced it. When he went to Chicago, she'd so wanted to go with him but couldn't leave her mother. For whatever reason, fate had deemed that the two of them were not destined to be together forever. Just for this summer. And the only ridiculous thought she had right this second was that they were wasting precious time.

"Yes, I'd like to double date."

"Okay. April wants to go, so that's what we'll do," Will declared.

"Good choice," Kim said. "I was about to play the man-of-honor card."

Will groaned. "You're going to make sure I regret saying yes to that, aren't you?"

Kim just smiled.

Thirty minutes later the four of them were sitting around a bistro table at Bar None. Delanie Carlson had taken their order of beers for the guys, white wine for the women and burgers all around. The place was packed and not only because it was Friday night. It was also summer and the tourists were out in force.

April watched Will make conversation with Luke. The high school football coach was a good-looking man with nearly black hair and brown eyes. He was physically fit, muscular, smart and completely crazy about Kim. Fortunately he was also a local boy and her friend wouldn't have to choose between the man she loved and the town that was woven into the fabric of her soul.

With a server in her wake, Delanie carried over a big tray. The two women set out drinks and food. "Anything else I can get you?"

"I don't think so," Kim answered.

"Okay. Enjoy. And just holler if you need anything."

"Thanks, Delanie," all four of them said together.

Her mushroom Swiss burger was as big as a Toyota, so April cut it in half, then took a bite. After chewing and swallowing she said, "I didn't realize how hungry I was. This tastes really good."

"It sure does." Will's eyes gleamed as if to say it didn't

taste as good as *she* did. Then the look faded and he turned his gaze on his sister's fiancé. "So, Luke, did you know that you're marrying a world-class meddler? As in my sister interferes in other people's lives."

"That's a little harsh," she defended. "I'm more of an idea person."

Luke didn't appear to be the least bit surprised or put out. "What did you do now, love of my life?"

"I came up with a brilliant plan. April's mission was to flirt with Will, have a thing for the summer, then be the one to end it before he goes back to Chicago. If she pulls that off, no one will feel sorry for her when he leaves."

Since everyone in town knew the story, April didn't bother going into her disastrous history with Will for Luke's benefit. "What Kim didn't factor in is that I'm not a skilled flirt. Give me a camera and I'm good. Give me a man and…" She shrugged as if to say "Insert appropriate slacker word here."

"I thought there was something wrong with her eyes at first," Will said.

The heated look he turned on April made her toes curl. "I tried to bat my lashes and it wasn't pretty."

"Yet here you two are," Luke pointed out. "So apparently my winsome and wonderful wife-to-be came up with an idea that had merit."

"And then some, my handsome, heroic husband-to-be." Kim looked at her man and raised an eyebrow. "He spent the night with her."

"Oh."

Will set the remaining half of his bacon cheeseburger down on his plate. "That's not the point, Luke. Before it's too late you should know that my sister is an epic interferer. And she's not likely to change, so beware. If she turns her powers on you, my friend, there could be hell to pay."

"Another way to look at it is that putting so much effort into the people she cares about is part of her charm," Luke said.

"Oh, my." April sipped her wine. "He's such a good man."

"I have to ask," Will persisted. "Does Tim know that you're going to side with his mom all the time?"

Luke laughed. "He does if he's as smart as I think he is."

"You've really got it bad," Will observed.

"Oh, you're so dramatic," Kim scoffed. "I bet you're really good when you go undercover."

Will's expression hardly changed, but there was something cold and intense in his eyes. "I try to do the best possible job whatever the assignment."

"I'm glad you appreciate me." Kim leaned over and kissed her intended's cheek. "My brother puts most of his energy into the police force. I wish he could find balance."

"Life and death, sis. That's the balance."

It didn't seem as if the other couple noticed, but April felt the shift in him, the darkness. He'd told her that dedication to his job had been responsible for his failed marriage, at least partially. And he'd also revealed that he'd married the wrong woman.

What if he married the right one? she thought. Would that balance him? Or was he unbalanceable?

She would probably never have an answer to that question because all he'd promised was a summer fling ending in a public breakup.

Will parked his SUV in the lot behind the sheriff's office and exited the vehicle. He looked at the spectacular blue sky and the towering Montana mountains and dragged in a deep breath of clean, fresh air, then grinned. This was the best he'd felt in probably years, a little carefree and a lot relaxed.

Sex with April no doubt had something to do with the relaxation. That particular tension had been gnawing at him since seeing her again. But it was even more than that. It was talking to her, being around her. Laughing. He hadn't realized how much he'd missed that. And dinner last night with Kim and her fiancé had been fun, and fun had been in short supply for a while now.

When he walked inside the office, Eddie and Clarice were already there. "Morning," he said.

"Hey, Sheriff." Clarice looked at him more closely. "You look perky today."

"Do I?"

"Yes, sir. Does it have anything to do with April Kennedy?"

"And why would you ask that?"

"Word around town is that the two of you were seen at Bar None last night," the clerk explained.

He really should have expected this. After all, his sister was the one who'd warned him to make sure the first time he saw April again was private and away from prying eyes. For some reason, today he couldn't muster the will to care that it was all over Blackwater Lake that he and April were dating. And under the conditions of their arrangement the more public their relationship, the more satisfaction April would get out of ending things.

"We were there last night," he admitted. "Had a great time with my sister and Luke. But you probably already know that, too."

His dispatcher smiled broadly. "That was brought to my attention, yes."

"Okay, then."

"I just made a pot of coffee, Sheriff," she said.

"I could use a cup." There was a table in the back of the room where the pot was kept along with supplies to keep it full. He walked back and grabbed one of the mugs sitting rim down and poured the hot black liquid into it. Clarice made it a point to wash up the mugs every day before she left and that was much appreciated.

Will walked back to her desk and leaned a hip on the corner. "What's up? Anything going on this morning that I should know about?"

"Pretty quiet. Got a complaint from out at the Harris place. During the night the barn was spray painted with words I refuse to repeat even though I know you've heard them all. Seems every summer we have to be the graffiti police. Eddie's going to check it out."

"Probably kids," the deputy said, joining him by the desk. "But I'll go out there and file a report."

"We'll need pictures. Do you want me to give April a call?" He wouldn't mind talking to her. Just hearing her voice always made him smile. Interesting because when she took pictures, she never told the subject to smile but clicked away while chatting with them, just capturing honest emotion.

"Sheriff?"

Will looked at the deputy. "Hmm?"

"I said I don't think it's necessary to bother April. This is the third call we've had with the same complaint. So far there's been no real evidence, but I'll take a couple pictures with my cell phone for the report. Just to be thorough. Unless someone catches them in the act…" Eddie shrugged.

Will nodded, then sipped his coffee. "Everything quiet at the campground out by the lake?"

During the summer there'd been a number of noise complaints. It was inevitable what with the campers living in close quarters. Usually too much alcohol was involved. But he'd instituted regular patrols because there was something sobering about a black-and-white sighting.

"Haven't had any calls, although it's still early," Clarice said. "But I think the drive-throughs make people stop and think. So far this summer the number of complaints from out there are down."

"Good." He looked at Eddie. "So when you're finished at the Harris place you'll swing by the campground?"

"Sure thing."

"Okay. Then I'll go catch up on paperwork—"

The ringing phone interrupted and Clarice answered. "Blackwater Lake Sheriff's Office, Clarice speaking. How can I help you?" She listened for several moments and the expression on her face changed from carefree to concerned. "How long since anyone has seen her? How old is she?" She jotted some notes then said, "I'll send someone right over."

"What's wrong?" Will asked.

"That was Mimi from the front desk at Blackwater Lake Lodge. There's a kid missing. Six-year-old girl. Been about an hour and a half since her parents saw her."

"Do you want me to go to the lodge first, Sheriff?" Eddie asked.

"No. I'll go." He set his half-empty mug down on Clarice's desk. "By the time I get there she'll probably turn up."

But when he got there, she still hadn't been found. Will interviewed the parents and each thought she'd been with the other. He believed them. Another thorough search of the property under his supervision was conducted without success.

Then he considered his options as a law-enforcement officer. This wasn't a custody dispute situation and after interviewing the staff there was no evidence of anyone or anything suspicious. That meant he couldn't make a case that the little girl was in imminent danger, which would meet the criteria for issuing an Amber Alert.

For now he would keep the search confined to the town of Blackwater Lake and the immediate area surrounding it. The parents had a recent picture of the little girl, Riley Shelton, and a description of the clothes she was wearing when last seen. Will assured them that everything possible would be done to locate their daughter. He didn't use the word promise because a long time ago he'd learned that too many things were out of his control and he wouldn't give them false hope.

When he returned to the office, Clarice took the picture and description to April so she could scan it and make up fliers to distribute around town. Will made phone calls and organized volunteers to search.

Fifteen minutes after that call his father walked into the office. "Hey, Will."

"What are you doing here, Dad?"

"Cabot Dixon called me and said there's a little girl missing up at the lodge."

"Yeah." Things sure didn't move that fast in Chicago.

"I'm here because you need all hands on deck. I'm on medical leave, not an invalid."

Will nodded. "Glad to have you on this."

After that, men, women, teenagers, anyone who could showed up at the office. Will organized them into groups of two and three. He had maps of the surrounding area broken up into grids and assigned one to each group. Clarice made sure each one had a cell phone and water.

The office door opened and April came in with a stack of papers and put them on the dispatcher's desk. "Here are the fliers."

Will picked one up and looked at the blue-eyed, blonde, freckle-faced little girl last seen wearing denim shorts and a lavender T-shirt with two characters from the movie *Frozen* on the front. "These are great."

"I already put one up in the window of my shop. Is there anything else I can do?" she asked.

He looked around the room, which was now nearly filled with volunteers who were grabbing up the fliers. "I'm going to assign one of the volunteers to take some of these and distribute them to the business owners around town. Then I'll head out and keep looking. I think we've got it covered for now."

"Those poor parents must be frantic with worry."

"Yeah." Will had seen that look too many times. Chicago or Blackwater Lake, it didn't matter. The fear was the same. But he would rather see that than grief and despair if they didn't locate this child.

Her eyes were full of concern. "I can't even imagine how they feel."

"I know."

"You'll find that little girl. I'm sure of it." She put a hand on his arm.

The warmth of her fingers felt good, reassuring, but he wasn't so sure about the success of this operation. Where he worked, too many kids didn't get a break. It was hard not to think the worst.

"We'll do our best," he said.

She nodded. "I'm thinking good thoughts."

"Okay. Thanks." He took a flier. "I have to brief the volunteers before they head out, then get to my search area."

"Good luck." She gave him a reassuring smile, then left the office.

Will stood by the dispatcher's desk and looked around the nearly filled-to-capacity room. "I need everyone's attention."

Almost instantly chatter stopped and you could have

heard a pin drop. "You all have your assignments. I need you to call in every hour whether you have news or not. Clarice will be here coordinating communication. Everyone stay together. We don't want anyone else lost out there."

"What if we find her?" one of the teenage girls asked.

"Call into the office and let Clarice know your position. She'll dispatch emergency personnel to you." He looked around again. "Any other questions?" When everyone shook their heads he said, "Thank you all for your help. Now, let's get out there and find Riley."

Will headed back out to the lodge and one more time searched the grounds immediately around the building, then expanded his perimeter, driving slowly. She was so little, he thought, and could be almost anywhere. He was alert to any flash of color and fervently wished she'd put on something that morning the color of the vests that construction and road employees wore to be visible.

He parked the SUV at the lodge and followed the paths on the grounds, trying to guess which way a curious six-year-old would go. What would attract her attention?

Just beyond the lodge property trails there was a clearing in the dense trees and underbrush. From here you could see some of the tallest mountains in Montana, where the very top had snow all year round. Will remembered Riley's mom telling him what she was wearing that morning, nerves compelling her to add that the characters were sisters from her favorite movie. One of them froze everything and went to the snowy mountains in order not to hurt anyone.

What if…

After calling dispatch to check in with Clarice and give her his position, he started walking toward the mountain. The trees quickly closed in and a child could easily become disoriented. Will had hiked and camped in here with his dad and knew the area well.

Every ten minutes he stopped and called out. "Riley? I'm a police officer. Can you hear me?" Then he'd carefully listen for a response.

For about an hour he kept at it, then checked in with the office for an update. Clarice had no news and the bad feeling that he always carried around with him got a little bit worse. That drove him on.

"Riley?" He listened. "It's Sheriff Fletcher. Can you hear me?" He stopped talking and listened again. There was a noise off to his right that didn't belong in the woods. He moved slowly in that direction. "Riley? I'm here to help you."

He heard the sound again. It was like whimpering, and exhilaration pumped his adrenaline. "Riley, honey, make some noise. Let me know where you are. I want to take you back to your mom and dad."

"Over here."

The words were faint and Will had trouble judging the direction. "Louder, honey. Shake the bushes so I can see where you are."

He heard her and moved steadily toward the sound. Finally he saw a flash of lavender and blond hair through the trees. Thank God. She was shaking a blackberry bush for all she was worth.

He moved beside her and went down on one knee. "Hey, Riley. My name is Will. Good job with that bush and helping me find you."

"I'm scared." Her mouth trembled.

"I bet you are. Don't worry. I'm here to help you." He gave her a quick once-over. "Are you hurt?"

"A little." She pointed to scratches on her shins. There

were some on her face, too, along with streaks where tears had tracked through the dirt. "I want my mommy."

"You got it, kiddo. But first, are you thirsty?"

"And hungry."

"I don't have food, but you'll be back at the lodge pretty soon and we'll get you something to eat. Here's some water." He took an unopened water bottle from the holder at his waist. When she'd had enough, she handed it back. He smiled at her, trying to put her at ease. "I like your shirt."

She nodded and looked down at her front, pointing to the blonde character wearing a long sparkly turquoise dress. "That's Elsa. She made everything frozen and thought she hurt her sister, Anna, so she went to the mountains where she couldn't hurt anyone ever again."

"Is that what you were doing when you wandered away? Trying to get to the snow on the mountain?"

She hesitated, then nodded. "I hurt my brother, then I felt bad. I didn't think it was far, but then I walked and walked. My legs are really tired."

"Do you want to ride on my shoulders?" he asked.

She nodded. "I really want my mom."

"Roger that."

He called Clarice and instructed her to notify the parents that he was bringing Riley back to the lodge. Then he wanted her to notify fire department search and rescue and have them standing by to check her out, although she seemed to be in good condition. After that she should call the volunteers back in and cancel the missing child alert.

After finishing his orders and hanging up, he held out his arms. "Come on. I'll give you a lift."

The walk back, even with the little girl on his shoulders, was completed in half the time. As he approached, he noticed a crowd gathered on the lodge's rear lawn. The group included the Sheltons, the hotel's general manager, some of the volunteers including his dad and a photographer from the *Blackwater Lake Gazette*.

Will handed Riley into her mother's waiting arms and her father shook his hand. When that wasn't enough thanks for bringing his child back safely, the man bro-hugged him. Really, no words needed to be spoken; the expression in their eyes said how grateful they were to him for bringing their child back safe and sound.

It felt good, really good, to get a positive outcome. In Chicago detectives were called in when someone broke the law. At that point there was no prevention and all he could do was try and find justice. Nothing wrong with that, but today it didn't compare to what he was feeling. It had been a very long time since he'd experienced this kind of job satisfaction.

He didn't know what it meant and deliberately refused to analyze the feeling too closely, but all he could think about was talking to April. He wanted to tell her about his really good, totally awesome day, share the excitement with her.

The way he used to.

Chapter Ten

April got home from work later than usual. It had been an exciting day, in the best possible way. Crisis averted and all was well in Blackwater Lake.

After changing out of her work jeans, putting on pink shorts and a white spaghetti-strapped top, she walked barefoot to the kitchen. "Now my biggest problem is what to have for dinner," she said to herself.

She opened the refrigerator, hoping to find something for a meal, which would, in fact, be a miracle since she hadn't bought groceries in a while. Or maybe the food elves had provided provisions, but no such luck. There was some celery in the crisper along with nasty-looking lettuce, fuzzy tomatoes and a shriveled-up cucumber. That eliminated salad as a possibility. But she did have a half dozen eggs, some mushrooms and cheese that could be rescued.

The freezer wasn't very bountiful. Just vegetables that were more ice than anything else. A container of ice cream with about two tablespoons left and a bag of frozen peas she kept for muscle aches after a run.

She had two choices besides going to the grocery store, which wouldn't happen tonight. One—a trip to the Fletchers where she might throw herself on their mercy. Two—dry cereal because there was no milk. Will was probably at home, which was both good and bad news for the same reason.

She wanted to see him, but getting too attached was a bad idea. For her own good she was confined to quarters and needed to fend for herself.

"I guess it's dry cereal." She sighed and went to the pantry, pulling out the box of Cheerios. "Mental note—tomorrow grocery shopping."

She opened the top flaps of the box and unrolled the plastic inner bag, then grabbed a handful of toasted oats in the shape of an O. There was a knock on the kitchen's sliding glass door and she looked over. Will was standing there. The rush of pleasure she felt at the sight of him put a hitch in her breathing that nearly made her choke on the cereal. It was a really good idea to keep her distance, but she didn't have the willpower to send him away.

Spineless? She preferred to think of it as being neighborly.

Box in hand, she walked over to the door and unlocked it, then slid it open. He had a brown bag in his hands with the logo of the Harvest Café.

"Hi." She smiled and knew that the joy of it came from deep inside. "This is getting to be a habit."

Not necessarily a good one. It would be too easy to get used to seeing him every day.

"What is?"

"You coming to my back door with food to rescue me from starvation."

"And not a moment too soon," he said, eyeing the big yellow box in her hands.

"I love it for breakfast. And yeah, I know it's dinner time, but it's good now, too," she said. "Come in. If you're up for it, one thing I do have is a bottle of wine."

"Your survival instincts are something to behold," he teased.

"It's about priorities." She pulled two stemless wineglasses from the upper cupboard and an unopened bottle of Cabernet out of the pantry. "Wine comes from grapes, so you've got your fruit. It pairs with anything, including cereal."

"It does if you're not particularly fussy," he pointed out. "And apparently you're not."

"Nope." April grinned happily, already drunk on just the sight of Will Fletcher. It was really good to see him and she couldn't find the energy to remind herself why it was a bad idea to be this happy. "And think of it this way. If there's an alien invasion or some other sort of crisis, after a glass of Cabernet I really wouldn't care."

"You'll get no argument from me." He set the brown bag on the island and pulled out several cardboard to-go boxes.

"What have we got here?" She opened the containers and found meat loaf, mashed potatoes, green beans, Caesar salad and chocolate cake. Her mouth started to water. Then she looked at the smile on his face and her heart melted. "This is hands down my favorite thing from the café. How did you know?"

"I walked in and asked for two meals to go. Lucy Bishop, one of the owners of the place, wanted to know who the second one was for. When I mentioned your name, she told me what your favorite meal is."

"So she knows you're bringing me dinner. I guess you and I aren't a secret around town?"

"Good guess." He opened the bottle of wine with her electric opener. "Clarice mentioned us being at Bar None with Kim and Luke. So, all evidence points to the word being out."

People in this town tended to become invested in the current community romance. They were going to be bummed when April broke up with Will. But that was a problem for another day. They still had some summer left.

"I'll set the table while you supervise the wine breathing," she said.

"Okay."

Five minutes later they were sitting across from each other at her kitchen table with full plates and wine.

April took a bite of the meat loaf and sighed with enjoyment. "My taste buds are doing the dance of joy thanks to you. This is the second time today that you're a hero."

"That seems a little overstated. All I did was walk in the diner, order and pay. It really was nothing." He shrugged, a no-big-deal gesture.

"Modesty." She sighed at the creamy taste of the mashed potatoes. "It's the hallmark of a hero."

"That's the thing. I'm not a hero."

"There you go again." She pointed her fork at him. "What do you call finding that little girl, carrying her for miles out of the woods and back to her family?"

"My job."

"Modesty," she said again. "On the local news they're calling you the hometown hero. Must feel pretty awesome being the guy in the white hat."

"All I did was act on a hunch." He lifted one shoulder. "I got lucky."

"I think it was more than that, and finding her unharmed must have felt great."

He looked thoughtful for several moments. "You know what feels good?"

Memories of the two of them in her bed came to mind, but she knew that was not what he meant. "Tell me."

"There was a positive outcome today."

"Isn't that what I just said? You found that little girl and brought her home." She sipped her wine.

"It's more than that." There was an expression on his face that was boyish and carefree. "The community came together. People dropped what they were doing to assist in the effort to find a missing girl."

Holding her wineglass in both hands, she watched him as different looks moved across his handsome features. "It's just how folks in Blackwater Lake roll."

"I know, at least on some level. But it's been a while since I experienced that small-town spirit for myself. That sense of pulling together. In Chicago it so often feels like us against them."

"Must be hard."

"It is sometimes. I'm part of a team that investigates, builds a case of evidence that may or may not go to trial. That's up to the city attorney."

"So it can happen that you put in hours of work without any charges being brought?"

"Yeah. The end result is taken out of our hands." He looked at her for several moments, then continued eating.

"I bet that's frustrating."

Her mind was racing as she dug into her food. She wanted so badly to ask whether or not he was happy where he was. Every job had its pros and cons, and she didn't want to hear him say that being a detective for CPD was everything he'd ever dreamed it would be.

She finished the last bite of meat loaf and put her fork

down. "How about you just focus on the positive. Today you got the *W*."

"A win." He pushed his empty plate away. "The sheriff's office took the call, mobilized the community, handled the search. From beginning to end we ran the show and it felt good to see the operation through to a positive conclusion."

April held out her glass. "To happy endings."

"I'll drink to that." There was a crystal, bell-like sound when he tapped the rim of his glass to hers. "Everyone who took part is a hero. You for doing the fliers with Riley's photo. Clarice for sitting in the office taking calls, coordinating information. My dad for leading his group. And everyone else who showed up to walk an assigned grid and look for her."

"You left out yourself for finding Riley."

"I wouldn't have been able to look where I did if everyone else wasn't searching somewhere else."

"That's true." She decided his look of satisfaction would have to be enough. "It's really something to celebrate."

"It's more than that. I really wanted to share the good news with you. For old time's sake."

April watched a smile turn up the corners of his mouth. She'd seen him do that more than once since he'd come back to town, but this time she saw genuine pleasure and it actually reached his eyes. He looked younger, as if the problems of the world had lifted from his shoulders. For the first time since he'd started his temporary duty in Blackwater Lake she saw the old Will. The man she'd fallen in love with.

"I'm glad you came over." She was feeling so much more than that but didn't have the words to tell him. Instead she stood and walked around the table, then held out her hand to him. "How do you feel about taking this celebration into the bedroom?"

Just like that his eyes went smoky and hot. He took her fingers in his and slowly got to his feet. "That sounds like the best idea I've heard all day."

Side by side they walked down the hall. She looked up at him. "Would you do me a favor?"

"If I can."

"Would you wear your white hat?"

He grinned. "If I had one I'd be glad to."

"Can we pretend?" she asked.

"Anything you want."

Will took her in his arms and kissed her until she could hardly breathe. They *celebrated* more than once and this time he didn't get up and sneak back to his house.

He spent the night in her bed, like he had before everything fell apart between them. Just like old times, he'd said.

Unfortunately that was a shadow hanging over her. He was like the old Will and could crush her heart for the second time.

April felt something move against her and opened one eye.

Will.

He was spread out all over the bed, which meant he probably wasn't used to sleeping with someone. That pleased her. More than she wanted it to. Waking up beside him and watching him sleep was pretty awesome, too. He was so handsome, so unguarded that it made her ache inside. She honestly couldn't believe that he was here. If she couldn't see, touch and taste him, she'd chalk this up to imagination.

"Are you staring at me?" His voice was hoarse and scratchy from sleep.

"Your eyes are closed," she said. "How can you possibly know that?"

"I can feel you looking." One eye opened just a little. "What's wrong?"

"I look hideous. Now that I know you're awake I'm just waiting for you to jump up and run screaming from the room."

"You'll be waiting a long time. You look beautiful."

"That's a lie." She smiled. "But I'll take it."

"If you knew what was good for you, you'd be the one running away from me." The guarded look was back. "I'm no hero and you shouldn't look at me like I am."

"Yes, sir." She saluted. "And speaking of a run, I was planning one this morning."

"I know."

"How?" She sat up in the bed and clutched the sheet to her chest.

He grinned. "That's such a girl thing to do since I saw every beautiful, naked inch of you last night."

Yes he had and the words made her smile. "How did you know I was going to run today?"

"You do every other day." He sighed at her look. "My bedroom faces the alley."

"So you spy on me?"

"I keep an eye on your house," he clarified.

"Are you a stalker?"

"Maybe. But it takes one to know one." He lifted one eyebrow and the expression was decidedly accusatory.

She got his drift. "So, you know that morning I 'accidentally' ran into you it was actually deliberate."

"It's pretty hard to get anything past me."

"Because you're a hotshot detective. Yada yada." She made a face at him. "You know, smugness is not a very attractive quality in a person. Decidedly not heroic. And you only pieced that together in hindsight because I told you the truth."

"Maybe." There was a gleam in his eyes when he started pulling on the sheet. "Or maybe I suspected from the beginning because you were nicer to me than I had any reason to expect."

"Kind of like now," she said, holding tight to the five-hundred-thread-count material covering her breasts.

"When do you have to open the shop?"

The soft, sexy, seductive tone in his voice had tension and heat coiling in her belly, making her thighs quiver. "Noon. This is my late day." And a good thing, too, because she had a feeling this was going somewhere she wanted to follow. "When do you have to go into the sheriff's office?"

"I've got time."

She relaxed her grip and let him pull the sheet away. "Okay, then."

His eyes went dark with desire as he pulled her into his arms. "Your run will just have to wait."

"Schedules were made to be flexible."

April loved being loved by him and couldn't seem to get enough. Afterward he went back to his dad's house for a shower while she took one at hers. Barely forty-five minutes later he was back and had extra clothes in his hands.

"Mind if I leave these here?" he asked. "I still need a sanctuary from wacky wedding stuff."

"Kim's not really that bad, is she?"

"You saw the meltdown," he reminded her. "She's normally levelheaded, but when a wedding is involved apparently a woman becomes schizophrenic."

"I really hope you're not profiling brides," she teased.

"Not at all. I'm just making a case for having a drawer at your house."

Her heart skipped and her stomach fluttered, which apparently shut down all the early warning signals from her brain. "I think that can be arranged."

He grinned. "You just saved my life."

"And don't you forget it. Let's put those away." April went into the bedroom and cleared out a space in her dresser for his clothes. Then they went back to the kitchen and she asked, "Do you want some breakfast?"

"I was hoping you'd ask."

"What would you like?"

"Besides you?" The heated look flashed through his eyes for the second time that morning.

Be still my heart, she thought. "If eggs aren't okay, we'll be making a trip to the Harvest Café because I don't have much of anything else. Getting supplies in here is quickly becoming a priority. I have to start a list."

"Do you still make those enchiladas with the green chili sauce?"

She hadn't for a while. Mostly she'd made them for him because he liked it so much. That brought back memories of him coming over when her mom had a girls' night out. April would cook and they loved being alone. It was a preview of what their life together would be like and she'd looked forward to that so much. But it had only ever been a preview, because they never had a life together.

"April?"

"Yes." She shook off the dark memories and concentrated on right now. He was planning on spending a lot of time here and she would focus on enjoying it. "I can make the enchiladas. Anything else I should put on the list?"

"Not unless you take me with you to lug the bags and chip in for the groceries."

"Sounds like a deal."

"I'll clean off the table." He was looking at the take-out containers and plates still sitting there from last night. "We got a little distracted."

"I won't tell if you won't." She met his gaze and grinned, not the least bit sorry that the lingering mess was her fault. The truth was, all things being equal, she would do the same thing again. "I'll make omelets."

It was really tempting to just stand there and watch him. The play of muscles across his back and shoulders when he worked was mouth-watering. That black Chicago PD T-shirt pulled tight around his biceps could occupy her attention for hours. And don't even get her started on the way his butt looked in those worn jeans.

She'd given him space for some of his clothes and they were going food shopping, splitting the bill. This was one notch below actually formally agreeing to move in together. It felt natural and right, like it should have been the first time.

Better than she'd imagined it could be before she'd found out they wouldn't last forever.

But this time she had a safety net. The relationship had an expiration date and their Labor Day breakup appointment was coming faster than she wanted to think about.

That was a reminder, as if she needed it, that she'd better hold on to her heart with both hands.

Chapter Eleven

"Holy crap."

Will looked at the calendar on his desk in his office and whistled. It was already August. Time flew when you were having fun and he definitely was. Days were busy, filled with the routine problems of the summer tourist season when the population in Blackwater Lake doubled. Nights he spent at April's. It had been several weeks since she'd given him a drawer in the dresser and the empty space beside her in the bed.

Mostly they hung out in the middle, wrapped in each other's arms.

Too bad it couldn't last. And looking at the calendar he could see in black-and-white how short his time in town was. And more significantly, his time in her bed. It had been perfect. Had him thinking about things he hadn't for a long time. But they couldn't make it work before and the same issues still stood in the way. If he was being honest there was another one. He'd failed at marriage and taking another chance wasn't high on his list.

He could only make the most of the time he had left. And speaking of that, through his open door he saw April walk into the outer office. They'd ridden into town together this morning because her car was at McKnight Automotive for an oil change. It was just about quitting time for him, so she must have locked up her shop for the day.

Will shut down the computer, grabbed his keys from the desk drawer and walked out of his office, closing the door behind him. He met April in front of Clarice's desk.

"Hi." He leaned down to kiss her lightly.

"How was your day?" she asked.

Better now, he thought, but didn't say that out loud.

"Busy." He looked at his dispatcher, who was observing them and approving of what she saw if he didn't miss his guess. "Just ask Clarice."

The woman nodded. "A couple of car accidents. Drunk and disorderly on the beach at the lake. Illegal fireworks in a restricted area. Must have been left over from the Fourth."

"That's not good," April said. "It's been too long since we had a really soaking rain, and the hills and mountains are pretty dry. The last thing we need is a forest fire."

"That's for sure," Clarice agreed. "Dry lightning is dangerous enough. We don't need stupid humans messing up. There was a bad one about twenty years ago that came too close to Blackwater Lake for comfort."

"I remember." Will's dad was the sheriff and didn't come home for days because he was setting up detours and keeping curious spectators away for their own safety.

"That was before I moved here." April met his gaze. "But I came from Southern California and there were some scary fires there."

"The locals in this town watch out for the flakes who aren't paying attention." Will didn't say it out loud, but there was no way to prevent some nut job who waited for the perfect set of circumstances—windy weather, motivation, opportunity—and deliberately set a fire. But he'd meant what he said. "Folks are vigilant and pick up the phone if they notice suspicious behavior."

"They watch out for people in general," April said. "I'm a perfect example. Your family sure took my mom and me under their wing."

A couple years after the Kennedys moved in across the alley from him, Will *really* watched April. That old bedroom window of his was a great vantage point to observe the cute little girl who had suddenly grown up and blossomed when he wasn't looking.

Then he'd gone and messed it all up. In a million years he never would have expected to even kiss her again, let alone be invited into her bed. It was a relief to have a plan in place so he didn't hurt her like last time. They were enjoying each other with no strings attached. Although, for reasons he didn't really understand, turning that page on the calendar just now had put a knot in his gut.

"You ready to go?" he asked her.

"Yup. Oh, I almost forgot—" She met his gaze. "I talked to Tom McKnight and the car has to stay there. He noticed the timing belt was slipping and he had to order the part he needs. It could take a couple of days to come in."

"No problem."

Will wouldn't put it out there for the nosy woman in front of them to spread around town, but they were going to the same place. Heck, now that he thought about it, Clarice probably already knew that, too. His sister, father and nephew were aware that he wasn't sleeping under the same roof they were. Again he was relieved that there was a plan in place to save April from being pitied by her well-meaning neighbors.

"Let's roll," he said.

The phone on the dispatcher's desk rang and Clarice picked up. "Blackwater Lake Sheriff's Office, Clarice speaking. How can I help you?" She listened for several moments then frowned. "Where?" After writing something down, she said, "I'll send someone over to check it out."

"What's going on?" Will asked when she hung up.

"That was Jeannie Waterman. A couple of teenagers are acting suspiciously. In your neighborhood actually."

"Did she recognize them?"

"Yes, as a matter of fact. Doug Satterfield and Mike Hutak."

When law enforcement knew your name it wasn't a good thing and he recognized these two. He held out his hand for her notes. "I'll check it out since I'm going that way. See you in the morning."

"Bye, Clarice. Say hi to your hubby for me," April said.

"Will do."

They walked to the rear of the office and went out the back door of the building. Will's SUV was parked right there and he opened the front passenger door for April. After she climbed in, he shut the door and walked around to the driver's side.

He got in, then turned the key in the ignition. "I really hope Jeannie Waterman is overreacting. That it's a couple of boys just hanging out."

"Me, too." She flashed a grin. "I feel like a sidekick. Can I be yours?"

"My what now?"

"Come on, Will. Don't be a stick in the mud and go all law enforcement-y on me. Every hero has a person he can count on in a crisis. A sidekick. You have one in Chicago."

"Yeah. But I call him a partner."

"Same thing." There was pleading in her voice. "Please. Don't drop me off. That will cost you precious time."

He had to admit she was right about that. A minute either way could mean catching these kids—or not. But if they'd really done something wrong, they were probably long gone. "Okay, you can come with me. But stay in the car."

"It's hard to be an efficient sidekick from the right front seat of a vehicle," she protested.

"Take it or leave it."

"You're very bossy," she said.

In the part of town where Will and April lived the houses fronted well-traveled streets with an alley in back for the garage. Unless these kids were complete idiots, that's where they'd be pulling their crap. So, he drove slowly up and down the back ways near the address Clarice had given him.

"There," April said, pointing.

Will didn't see anything. Hedges in this area were nice for privacy, but could easily hide mischief in progress. "What did you see?"

"Believe it or not, an egg went flying through the air." She peered steadily through the front window then pointed again. "There," she said again.

"Okay. I saw it." He pulled the SUV to a stop several houses away. "Stay in the car. I mean it."

He got out quietly, then soundlessly picked his way to the hedge that was almost as tall as he was. He peeked around it and sure enough the teens in question had egged the car in the driveway and were working on the garage door. Parked just two houses down was a beat-up old truck that he knew belonged to the sixteen-year-old Satterfield kid. Hutak didn't have a driver's license yet.

Will walked into the open and stopped in the best place to block their exit if necessary. "Hey, boys."

They both whirled around and the younger one dropped the cardboard egg carton in the driveway, breaking the few that were left. The two of them looked guilty as sin.

"Don't even think about making a run for it. I know where you live."

"Are you going to arrest us?" Hutak was skinny, blond and scared.

"Maybe." Will watched their body language for any sign of running. "You want to tell me why you did this? You got a beef with someone who lives here?"

"Maybe." Satterfield had black hair and eyes with an attitude to match.

Will didn't miss the fact that the kid threw his own words back at him. "Smart ass."

He shrugged. "Or maybe we were bored."

That was probably more like it, Will thought. "Well, before I call your parents, you're going to be busy cleaning up the mess you made."

"No way—"

Will held up a hand to stop Hutak's protest. He liked these two for the profanity-laced graffiti on the barns, too. "Before your mouth writes checks you can't cash, I've got another question. If I search that truck of yours, Satterfield, am I going to find cans of spray paint?"

The two exchanged another guilty glance. "That's what I thought," he said. "Seems like you're going to have a lot to do for the rest of the summer painting over the stuff on the barns you vandalized."

"You can't make us," Hutak said.

"You're right about that," Will agreed pleasantly. Behind him he heard the sound of sneakers and figured his "sidekick" had disobeyed orders. "But I can make the alternative to it feel like the lowest level of hell. Now let's get this mess cleaned up before it dries and you're looking at charges."

He marched the boys to the back door and a woman he didn't know answered. After he calmed her down and explained the boys needed soap, water and rags to undo what they'd done, she was more than happy to oblige and leave him to supervise them.

Satterfield hosed eggshells and slime off the garage and car. "Slave labor is against the law, you know."

"This is more in the neighborhood of punishment fitting the crime." Will folded his arms over his chest.

"You're not really going to call my parents, are you?" Hutak was looking pretty sorry for himself. "If you do, I'm never going to get my driver's license. I'm not even going to have time to learn to drive because I'll be grounded for the rest of the summer."

"Look on the bright side. You'll only be grounded when you're not painting barns," Will said. He heard laughter from behind him.

"My life is over," Hutak said to his friend. "I'm never listening to you again."

"You're such a candy-ass." But Satterfield didn't sound quite as defiant anymore.

When they'd finished, returned the cleaning supplies and apologized to the woman, Will called the parents. Within ten minutes both sets showed up. None of them gave him any excuses for their sons' behavior. They expressed regret and appreciated him taking the time to teach the kids a lesson, saying they had the situation from here.

After they left he joined April in the SUV. "You didn't stay in the car."

"In sidekick school you'd flunk out for not backing up

the hero." She didn't look intimidated like the teens. "I was making sure you didn't need help."

And speaking of help, the parents of those kids had thanked *him* for helping their children. He'd responded that he'd been happy to do it. Just now he realized that was the honest-to-God truth. It was the second time in the past few weeks that he'd found satisfaction in doing his job.

He shouldn't get used to the feeling. Since he'd arrived, he never missed an opportunity to remind people his status was temporary.

His sidekick was temporary, too, besides being a whole lot cuter than his partner in Chicago. And wasn't that a bitch and a half.

Will wasn't quite sure how his dad had talked him into going fishing on his day off, but here they were at the Blackwater Lake Marina. He parked his SUV in the paved lot and they both got out. Just up the small rise he saw the house where the previous owner had added on an upstairs apartment to rent out. Jack Garner owned the whole property now and word was he used one unit for an office and lived in the other one. Just then the bestselling author walked out the front door following after the ugliest dog Will had ever seen.

Jack glanced over, lifted a hand in greeting, then headed in their direction. He stopped in front of them and shook hands. "How are you, Hank?"

"Better. Best shape of my life according to my daughter." He bent to pet the dog's homely, hairy head. "What kind of dog is this?"

"Chinese crested. Harley, say hello." He grinned when the dog barked.

Will stared at the skinny creature that was hairless, except for his head, tail and paws. "Seems...good-natured."

Jack met his gaze and there was something just shy of warning in his dark eyes. "That's like telling a woman she has a good personality. I know he's not the handsomest canine in the kennel, but he picked me out. And I wasn't even looking for a dog." Harley took off. "We're finished being neighborly. Gotta go."

"The writer doesn't waste words." His dad watched Jack follow his dog around the lake.

"I guess you've met him before," Will said.

"Yeah. In town. Never met the dog, though." He shook his head. "Let's go fishing."

They walked up a couple of steps and into the marina store. Brewster Smith was putting Summer Clearance signs on the racks of T-shirts, tank tops, bathing suits and lightweight jackets. Will didn't much appreciate the reminder that summer was quickly coming to an end.

It meant saying goodbye to April and he was nowhere near ready to do that. She was sunlight and magic and heat. Chicago winter was gray and dark and cold. Who wouldn't want to stay here longer?

"How are you, Brew?" Hank greeted the other man.

"Dandy, thanks. You're looking fit as a dang fiddle." He checked Hank out from head to toe. "Recuperation agrees with you."

"That it does."

"How you doin', Sheriff?"

Will shrugged. "Can't complain."

"How's that nephew of yours?"

"He's a great kid." Thanks to everyone but him, Will thought, because he'd been career focused. "Kim's done an amazing job with him. And she couldn't have done it without Dad."

Hank nodded. "I wouldn't have chosen this path for her,

but I couldn't be prouder of the way she handled a difficult situation. And she gave me my grandson."

"Now she's getting married. The years sure have gone by fast." Brew shook his head in amazement. "How's the weddin' stuff coming along?"

"Good," Will answered. "I guess."

Hank laughed. "If you spent more time at the house instead of escaping to April's every night, you'd know for sure that all is well. And you're her man of honor." Before Brewster could ask, he added, "That's like a maid of honor except a man is doing the honor stuff."

Brewster rubbed a hand across the full beard on his chin. "I'm not sure what to say about that except that you'll look fetching in the dress."

"Very funny." Will was glad he'd picked that to comment on and not his relationship with April. He didn't want to put a finer point on what was going on with them.

"I'm a regular comedian." Brew grinned. "So you're spendin' a lot of time with our favorite photographer?"

So much for dodging the subject. "We're friends."

"Hmm." The older man looked at his dad. "You buying that?"

"I stay out of things unless invited in," Hank said.

"Fair enough." The other man looked from one to the other. "What can I do for you fellas today?"

"Going fishing," Hank said. "We need to rent equipment and a rowboat."

"How come you don't have your own?" Brewster asked.

"Never had time. Now I'm recuperating." He looked at Will. "We need two rods, tackle, lures and the whole nine yards. And that rowboat. I'll handle the oars. It's part of my cardiac rehab."

"Good," Will said.

"Okay, then."

Brewster gathered a couple of fishing rods and a tackle box with everything they'd need, then wrote up a receipt and took Will's credit card for all charges. They carried everything to the slip on the dock where the boat was tied up and his dad rowed them out of the marina and to a place not far away that most tourists didn't know about. Cutter's Cove was a locals' secret and shared only with a trusted few out-of-towners. Hank stopped and stowed the oars, then each of them took a rod and got it ready. In a few minutes they'd dropped their lines, then sat in companionable silence.

Will adjusted the baseball cap he wore and looked up at the blue sky. Not a single cloud to break up the expanse—only the mountain peaks did that. The surface of the water was like blue glass while birds chirped and called overhead and from trees on the shore. He let out a breath and with it went a whole lot of accumulated tension.

"This was a great idea, Dad."

"Thought you could use it, son." Hank reeled in his line, then cast it out again in an easy, experienced single movement of his wrist.

"Yeah. I've missed this."

"How's the job going?"

"Good, I'd say. Why?" He looked at his dad. "Are people complaining about me and begging you to come back?"

"No." He laughed. "It's just you haven't said much. I'm feeling a little guilty for pulling you away from big city detective work. Do you miss it?"

Did he? Will hadn't really thought about it. His time and energy had gone into taking care of Blackwater Lake and...

April.

"It's not a good sign when that much time goes by without an answer."

Will looked at his father, who was also wearing a baseball hat and aviator sunglasses. Even with all his detective experience he couldn't tell what this man was thinking. And he didn't know how he felt, but his dad hadn't asked him to compare and contrast his job in Chicago with the one here in Blackwater Lake. So he'd decided to focus on how the current assignment was going instead of whether or not he missed his job in Chicago.

"I helped two teenagers see the error of their ways," he started. "Caught them in the act of egging a car and they pretty much admitted spray painting barns because they were bored."

"Yeah. Heard that before."

"I bet you have." Will grinned. "The cool thing is that I got their confession while making them clean up their mess."

"Very badass of you, son."

"I'm glad you approve." Will chuckled, then his amusement disappeared as he thought about what might have happened in CPD jurisdiction. His dad hadn't asked him to compare and contrast, but he did automatically. "I didn't have to arrest those kids and start a paper trail that could follow them for a long time. There were no loopholes in the law or plea deals with a prosecutor that put dangerous people back on the street who should stay locked up."

"We're not talking Blackwater Lake now, are we?"

Will sighed, but all he said was, "Justice and punishment aren't so swift and tidy in Chicago. Here I made a difference on a basic level. I made a positive difference in two lives and didn't have to jail a couple of juveniles and put them in the system. That carries a lot of satisfaction for me. I called their parents and something tells me that will be enough."

Hank nodded thoughtfully. "If they reoffend, you won't know. You'll be back in Chicago."

He waited to feel the thrill of excitement at the thought of going back, but it never came. Without much enthusiasm he said, "Yeah."

Hank set his fishing rod in the bottom of the rowboat and braced it against the side, then reached into their rented cooler filled with ice and pulled out two cold bottles of water. He handed one to Will.

"Is it possible that you're experiencing job burnout?"

"I don't know."

Will liked being a detective. Putting forensic evidence together with witness statements and interviews to come to a conclusion and take a bad guy off the street. It was a satisfying career. At least it had been. But since coming back home, he'd seen that there were holes in his life, gaps that he'd been successfully able to ignore for a long time.

An image came to mind of the pleasure on April's face when he was buried deep inside her. Her beautiful dark hair spread over the rose-print pillow case. Their naked bodies pressed together, becoming one. It was going to be hard to walk away from her. And he'd seen for himself how people cared about their *favorite photographer*. In the end, she would dump him and avoid the town pity party. But in Chicago, no one would give a damn that he'd been publicly put in his place. He opened the bottle and took a long, cold drink.

"The thing is, son, that heart problem I had made me realize a lot of things."

"I bet," Will said. "Anything specific?"

"Yeah. How much I love my family and that I'd like to be around for a while. I'm willing to go along with the good Lord's plan when He's ready to take me, but I can't think of any reason to make it easy on Him, or go sooner than necessary."

"You're taking care of yourself now," Will said. "Eating right and exercising."

"There's something else." Hank rested his elbows on his knees and dangled the water bottle between them. "I'm giving a lot of thought to retiring."

"Makes sense." But Will remembered his dad talking about this and knew where he was going.

"I think so. The thing is, though, I want to leave the town in good hands. Your hands, son."

"You can find someone better than me," he said.

Here's where the compare-and-contrast thing went the other way. In Chicago the system was so big that the general population had no clue what went on unless it was breaking news. You put your nose to the grindstone and worked hard. In Blackwater Lake it was personal. If he let people down, they were friends and neighbors.

"I don't think there is anyone better," Hank said. "Folks know and trust you because you were born and raised here."

"That doesn't automatically qualify me to be the best person for the job. What about Eddie?"

His father snorted. "He's smart and eager, but young and green. He could grow into the job but not soon enough. And I believe you have more experience and training."

"Even if I wanted to do it, don't folks get a vote?"

"There would be a special election, but half the people in town won't even know it isn't me on the ballot."

"Yeah," Will said wryly, "because we look so much alike."

"Actually, I'm better looking," his father teased.

This was a lot to think about. That day he'd gone to Mercy Medical Clinic with his father for the checkup, his dad had hinted that this was coming. Now that he'd voiced it to the universe, Will couldn't ignore the subject any longer.

"I don't know about this, Dad." He waited for the same arm-twisting guilt trip his sister had put on him when his father ended up in the hospital before the surgery.

"Just one more thing, son." His father took off his sunglasses and there was a look in his eyes impossible to ignore. "I know you always wanted a career in law enforcement since you were a little guy. As you grew up it became clear that you didn't want to do that in my shadow, so Chicago was where you set your sights. And you've done that. I'm real proud of you, Will. Always have been and always will be."

That meant a lot to him. Will made every decision by asking himself whether or not it would make his dad proud or disappointed in him.

"Thanks, Dad."

"Just think about the sheriff's job, Will. Maybe it's something you didn't even realize you want."

Will waited for more, hoping to have something to get defensive about. He should have known better because that had never been his dad's style.

Damn it.

Chapter Twelve

April thought Kim was surprisingly calm considering this was her wedding day. She'd gotten dressed at the Blackwater Lake Lodge where the ceremony and reception would take place soon. This suite was where she would spend her first night with her new husband. Her family was all here: the man of honor, her dad and son.

It was April's job to take candid photos, so that's what she was doing. Trying to be like a fly on the wall and not attract notice. She was constantly adjusting the lens and depth of field to bring one or another of the Fletchers into sharp relief while blurring the background of the shot. The four of them were laughing, teasing, joking. *Family.*

Something April had longed for all her life. But no matter how much she wished it could be different, she was on the outside looking in. And that sounded pathetic. She didn't mean it to be. Her best friend was happy and April couldn't be more pleased.

She took some random shots of the suite's living room with its sofa, love seat, and mahogany coffee and end tables. There was a wet bar and small kitchenette with microwave. A doorway led to the bedroom, which she knew looked like a tornado had hit it. There were pictures as proof. It was important to her that Kim have photographic evidence of every part of this day, even the untidy parts because that's what made the memory real.

When her view was suddenly blocked, she lowered the camera. Will was standing in front of her looking so handsome in his traditional black tuxedo. *Be still my heart*, she thought, then adjusted her own attitude the way she would a lens on her camera. It was important he not know how profoundly he affected her.

"You need a break," he said. "Stand down for a few minutes. It's going to be a long night."

"But I might miss the perfect shot," she protested.

"If you do, no one will ever know. Put down the camera."

"Or what, Sheriff?"

"I'll have to take you in." His voice was slightly north of normal, tipping into seductive territory.

"That could be interesting." But she set down her camera on the coffee table.

Behind them came the sound of metal on glass. Kim was signaling for attention. Her blonde hair hung to her shoulders in layers that framed her pretty face. A crystal-encrusted comb secured the veil that hung to the middle of her back. She looked like a princess in her full-skirted white gown with the lace bodice, sweetheart neckline and cap sleeves.

"I'd like to make a toast if someone will open the champagne."

"I can handle that." Hank twisted off the metal wire on

the mouth of the bottle, then used his thumbs to pop the cork. After pouring some into five flutes, he handed them out, including one for April. He looked at his grandson. "Just a sip for you."

"I know, Granddad." But the teenager looked eager.

As Kim held up her glass, the emotion in her eyes bordered on tearful. "In this room is everyone I love."

"What about Luke?" Will asked.

"Everyone except Luke, smart aleck. I wouldn't be here without you guys." She looked at each of them. "Here's to all of you. Especially to Will for carrying a bouquet when he walks down the aisle in front of me."

"To Will," they all said.

"They" included everyone *but* Will. "I'm not drinking to the bouquet part of that toast, only to the love and walking down the aisle in front of you part. And, in my opinion, that's going above and beyond the call of brotherly duty."

"It wouldn't hurt you to get in touch with your feminine side," Kim teased.

"Are you sure about that?" Will asked. "It could be psychologically damaging to me. Therapy's looking pretty attractive right now."

"Oh, man up, Will." Kim grinned at him.

"That's the problem," he said, clearly enjoying the pushback. "It's bad enough that you talked me into filling a traditionally female role in your wedding, which, by the way, goes against all the rules of manhood. Then you spring this bouquet thing on me in a family toast. That's very underhanded, by the way. I draw the line at carrying flowers. It's just not manly."

"Really, Will—" Kim tsked.

"Dad, help me out here." He looked from his father to his nephew. "Tim?"

"You're on your own, dude." The teen shrugged. "She's my mom. I'm not stupid."

"Okay. I understand." Will nodded. "I get the parent/child bond. So, Dad, feel free to jump in here anytime and back me up on this."

"Well, son—" There was a twinkle in his father's eyes. "The things we don't want to do are usually the ones that build character."

"Since when is a wedding a teachable moment?" Will looked at his family. "It's a conspiracy. I'm ashamed of you guys." He met April's gaze. "I know my sister is your best friend, but you're sensible. Probably the only one in this room besides me who is. You don't think I should carry flowers down the aisle, do you?"

Four pairs of eyes belonging to the people she cared most about in the world were watching her. She knew this whole silly conversation was a tension reliever for the bride, who in five minutes would descend the lodge staircase and take her vows. The Fletcher family didn't take it lightly. Will had told her as much when confessing his own feelings of failure about his marriage. Kim intended to only do this once, hence the tension.

So, April responded in the spirit of fun. "Come on, Will. You face armed criminals without batting an eye. It's flowers, not pantyhose, high heels and a tiara."

All of them stared at her for a moment, then cracked up. Will laughed the hardest.

Kim waved her hand in front of her eyes. "Laughing till you cry is still crying. I'm going to ruin my makeup."

Just then there was a knock on the door and Hank opened it. Hadley Michaels, Blackwater Lake Lodge's manager and events coordinator, stood there. She had auburn hair and turquoise eyes. In her navy jacket, skirt and matching low-heeled pumps she exuded an air of prim and proper that was far more mature than she should be at twenty-six. "Five minutes, everyone. We need to get you all in the staging area. There's a schedule to maintain."

April grabbed her camera and followed the others out the door of the suite, snapping pictures of their backs as they walked down the hall to the elevator.

Will took his sister's hand and tucked it into the bend of his elbow. "I'm drawing a line in the sand. No bouquet carrying."

She touched the white rosebud boutonniere on his jacket. "Okay, but you could pull it off no problem. Next to Luke, you're the manliest man I know."

The tender brother/sister moment brought tears to April's eyes. Fortunately the lens didn't have emotions to cloud the issue and clearly captured the moment for posterity.

They rode down to the second floor and April got out first, then backed up to take pictures. She got one of them lined up at the top of the stairs with Will waiting to lead everyone down.

She looked at him. "Okay, give me a couple of minutes to get in position."

Will winked at her. "Roger that."

Something about the way he looked, the man himself, slammed her heart and her first thought was, *This can't be.* Anything more than friendship was against the rules. But when she hurried downstairs, the area around the fireplace was filled with friends who were there to wish Kim and Luke every happiness in their married life. Weddings were a seething cauldron of emotion and that's why she'd suddenly been overwhelmed with feeling something deeper for Will. It would pass.

She focused on the minister and Luke, who were waiting in front of about thirty people sitting in folding chairs set out for the event. To the left was a trio of female musicians, one on violin, another playing the flute and a harpist. There were flowers everywhere—roses, lilies, baby's breath. It smelled like a garden and her only regret was that her camera couldn't capture the wonderful, sweet scent.

April did a quick pan around the room to capture the spectators, knowing Kim wouldn't be able to take it in now. Then the trio started the wedding march and the bride began her stairway descent with her brother in the lead and flanked by her father and son. She adjusted her lens and settings to get close-ups of their expressions, then pulled back to take in the flower garland and white bows decorating the banister.

April moved quickly to get a signature shot. Everyone was looking at the bride and she wanted to capture the expression on her groom's face when he got his first glimpse of the woman who would be his wife. Money shot, she thought, snapping the exact moment Luke looked dazzled, happy and head over heels in love. Then she zoomed in on Kim's face filled with absolute joy at the sight of the man she was about to marry.

Will was first down the aisle between the chairs and took his place beside Reverend Owen Thurmond from the nondenominational church in Blackwater Lake. The pastor was in his midforties and had kids who went to the local high school where the bride and groom worked.

Then Hank and Tim escorted Kim down the aisle, stopping right where they were supposed to.

The pastor asked, "Who gives this woman to be married to this man?"

Hank smiled lovingly down at his daughter, then kissed her cheek. He nodded at his grandson before meeting the minister's gaze. "Her son and I do."

Luke moved closer, held out his hand and her father

tucked his daughter's fingers into it, into the safekeeping of her husband-to-be. They walked the several steps and stood facing the minister.

"We are gathered together in the sight of God to join this man and this woman in marriage. I think I speak for the whole town of Blackwater Lake when I say that in terms of finding a soul mate right under your nose, it took you two long enough."

"We needed a little push," Kim said, blowing a kiss to her son, who now stood beside the minister in the best-man spot.

"I don't have to tell you both that marriage is an institution of respect because the fact that you waited so long for the right person speaks to your high regard."

April happened to have her lens on Will and pressed the shutter. For just a moment there was a look in his eyes that she now knew was about his regret at the failure of his own marriage.

"Still," the minister continued, "relationships are like a garden—pleasing at first bloom but eventually needing attention to maintain its lush beauty. In other words it needs work." He looked at each of them. "I understand you've written your own vows?"

"We have," Luke said.

Kim held out her bouquet to Will and shrugged. "I swear holding this is in the job description."

"Okay." He gave her a grin.

April took multiple shots of that, wishing some of the criminals he'd put away could see the badass detective in touch with his feminine side.

Kim had unfolded a sheet of paper and started to read. "Please indulge me in my cheat sheet but I was afraid nerves would make me draw a blank. I'm only doing this once and wanted the vows to be as perfect as I could get them." She turned and smiled at her groom. "On top of that pressure, there's also the fact that I teach English and I struggled to make my vows as eloquent as I urge my students to be. I wanted to do justice to what I feel in my heart. As much as I respect language, there are no words to tell you how much I love you. But I promise to show you every day how deeply I care. I will support you and take care of you the best way I know how. And I will go to every football game, and cheer for you and the team more enthusiastically than anyone else."

Luke laughed but his eyes were suspiciously bright, which would be a fantastic picture. "I'm a football coach, which makes me competitive, so I memorized my vows. Not the best game play because, Kim, you're so beautiful that I'm at a loss for words. I've completely forgotten what I planned to say." There was a chorus of laughter and *awws* from the guests. "But here's the substance of it. I'm the luckiest man in the world. I promise to be the best husband possible and a father to your son. I love him as if he were my own. And I love you. I will cherish you as long as I live. And yeah, I'm going to put a spin on the traditional vows because I promise to obey."

"Brave words, Luke." The minister chuckled along with the guests looking on. "May the spirit of your words as you promise to love each other sustain you throughout your life together. Do you have the rings?"

"I do." Will smiled, then said, "Yes."

Owen took them and gave the smaller one to Luke. "Do you take Kim to be your wife?"

"I do." He slipped the simple band on her left ring finger.

"Kim, do you take Luke to be your husband?"

"I do." Her hands trembled as she slid the band on Luke's finger. Then he took her hands in his to steady them.

"It's official." Owen looked at everyone gathered to witness the ceremony. "I present to you Mr. and Mrs. Luke Miller. Luke, you may kiss your bride."

When he did, the spectators stood and applauded. April captured everything she could, but found she kept straying back to Will. She reminded herself to be professional. Newlyweds first, family second. But her eye kept searching out Will.

Because he would be gone soon and she wouldn't be able to search him out at all.

"This dress cost me blood, sweat and tears, not to mention sleep," Kim said to her new husband. "I'm not taking it off."

"No, that would be my job now." Luke smiled, a suggestive look in his eyes.

April was standing right there at the edge of the dance floor where they'd had their first dance as husband and wife. He'd made a comment about the impressive circumference of her gown and the challenges of navigating it gracefully. She continued to snap pictures and got the laughter, love and intimacy after this brief back-and-forth. Now the new Mr. and Mrs. were working the room, which was beautifully decorated with white linens on the tables, flowers and flameless candles everywhere. In the corner, a table for wedding gifts was full and people had put presents on the floor surrounding it.

She was looking around for more candid shots of people sitting at the circular tables chatting while some couples were making their way to the dance floor when the DJ started playing a slow song. She noticed two of the Fletcher men walking purposefully toward her. Since she was alone, the two of them probably had something to say to her.

"Hank," she said, then looked at Will. "Hi, great party."

"Yeah. It's a shame you're missing it. But Dad and I came up with a plan to fix that."

"I don't want to hear this, do I?"

"Probably not. But we don't really care." Hank looked at his son. "Tell her, Will."

"Coward." But he grinned. "Okay. Everyone has eaten but you, missy."

"Missy? What are you? The food police?" She shrugged. "Sorry. Couldn't help it."

"You're hilarious," Will said. "As it happens we've been deputized by the bride, who wants you to take a break and eat. She said to tell you it's selfish on her part. If you don't keep your strength up the pictures won't be any good."

April laughed. "That sounds like her. But—"

"I know what you're going to say. And if you trust me with your camera," Hank said, "I can fill in. If they're not good you can work your Photoshop magic on them."

She stared lovingly at the camera in her hands, then gave him an apologetic look. "It's really expensive. Not that I don't trust you—"

"But you don't. I understand." Hank slid his hands into the pockets of his tuxedo slacks.

"I have a compromise. There's an inexpensive point-and-shoot in my equipment bag on that chair in the corner. Would that be okay?"

"A relief, actually. That one—" he indicated the bulky, impressive apparatus in her hands "—is too much responsibility for a rookie."

"Okay, then, it's settled," Will said. "I'll make sure she gets something to eat and you take over photography duties."

"Done." Hank headed over to where she'd pointed out her bag.

Will put his hand at the small of her back and guided her

to a table with one pristine setting left. The other places had wadded-up napkins, half-filled coffee cups and partially eaten slices of wedding cake. He sat her down, then signaled to one of the waitstaff to bring food. Moments later she had a Waldorf salad, petite filet, rice pilaf and asparagus.

"Looks yummy. I'm starving." She dug in to the salad, then started working on the rest. Will sat beside her and watched, a bemused look on his face. She chewed a bite of meat, then swallowed and said, "What?"

"You're really enjoying that."

"You bet. Best food in town here at the lodge." She ate the vegetable as he continued to stare. He was making her nervous in a sexy, take-me-to-your-bedroom way. So not appropriate right now. "Don't you have things to do, Mr. Man of Honor?"

"Yeah. The toast. But Kim wanted everyone fed and relaxed before that and the rest of the traditional stuff. So I don't have anything right now. Except take care of you."

"Babysitting me, you mean." There was a quiver in her tummy that had nothing to do with food and everything to do with *him*.

"It's a dirty job." He shrugged. "But someone has to do it."

"Wow. Feel the love," she said wryly.

In the next moment she wanted those words back. Their plan had evolved in order to avoid that messy *L*-word complication. No way she wanted to change the rules. But she wished he didn't look as tempting as sin. So very James Bond-y in his tux. And this being sweet to her just had to stop. None of that was part of their deal.

"Really, Will, you're part of the family and should go mingle."

"Those were not the orders given to me by the bride. I'm supposed to make sure you eat and have some fun."

When the word *fun* came out of Will's mouth all kinds of things came to mind, but not one of them would be suitable in a room full of people at a wedding reception.

She put down her fork. "I have to get back to work."

"Dance with me first." He touched a finger to her mouth when she started to protest. "You should be aware that I'm not taking no for an answer." When his nephew walked by, Will grabbed him. "Tim, watch April's camera."

"No sweat," the teen answered.

Will held out his hand to her and she only hesitated for a moment before she took it. After tugging her to her feet, he led her to the dance floor and slid an arm around her waist before settling her snugly against his big, hard body. There was nowhere on earth she would rather be, April realized, and she needed to savor every second since their time together would be over very soon.

She slid her arm around his neck and he rested his chin against her temple. In time to the slow song playing, he guided her around the floor and for a few minutes she could pretend they were alone. His heat and strength surrounded her and made a protective cocoon she wanted to stay in forever.

But when the music ended, so did her quiet moment. The DJ announced that all single ladies, regardless of age, should come out on the dance floor because the bride was going to throw the bouquet.

"I have to get my camera," she said.

Will blocked her exit. "You're single. Jean Luc doesn't count."

"No, I need to—"

He took her shoulders and turned her, then gently nudged her toward where Kim was standing with a growing group of females from eight to eighty. "Dad will get these pictures."

April moved toward the group and took a spot at the back. As the tradition went, whoever caught the bride's bouquet would be next to get married. The chances of that happening to her were about as good as a hookup with Jean Luc, she thought.

The DJ announced last call for the ladies before Kim took her place, turned her back and prepared to toss the flowers over her head. Flashes went off as the guests took pictures. Then the bride lowered her arm and turned toward the group of ladies.

"I hope everyone will forgive me," she said. "But I'm going to cheat." The women parted as Kim walked over to April and stopped. "You're my BFF. I want this day to be perfect, which by my definition means you have to have this."

"But, Kim—"

"No *but*s. I can't control everything. All I can do is make sure you get this. The rest is up to you." There was a determined look in her friend's eyes.

April sighed and took the flowers, then hugged her friend. "Luke's right. This dress has an impressive circumference."

"I'll take that as a thank-you."

"And so much more. I love you, my friend. You're going to be so happy."

"I love you, too. Thanks, and you're welcome." Kim pulled away and said, "Now Luke is going to throw the garter."

The DJ made the announcement and then the bride sat in a chair with her groom on one knee in front of her. She lifted her impressive skirt just enough for him to find the lacy garter with the powder-blue bow and slide it down her thigh and off. The single guys, including Will, gathered like the women had and the groom turned his back and tossed it over his head into the crowd.

A young guy beside Will grabbed it, then seemed to realize what he'd done and the ramifications of his athleticism. Horrified, he pushed the lace into Will's hands as if it were a hot rock.

"No way, man," he said, before quickly exiting the area.

Will walked over to April and studied the bouquet in her hands. "I think any superstition is null and void if the rules are bent to the breaking point."

"I'm sure you're right."

"Smile, you two." Hank was there with her less complicated camera. "I'm the acting official photographer. Ready? Say cheese."

Will let his dad snap a couple of photos while they stood side by side. Then he stuffed the garter in his pocket, took April in his arms and bent her back before kissing her soundly. Flashes went off around them, proving this impulsive act did not go unnoticed.

He met her gaze and his own was hot and bright. "Take that, tradition."

"You're just full of surprises," she said breathlessly.

The microphone crackled before the DJ said, "Listen up. The waiters are circulating to make sure everyone has a glass of champagne. It's time for the toast."

"That's my cue." Will pulled her upright.

April caught her breath and watched him head back to the bridal table. Pulling herself together with an effort, she retrieved her camera and thanked Tim for his excellent guardianship. Through her lens she watched and recorded Will's speech.

"Ladies and gentlemen, I hope you're having a great time." There was a round of applause and he smiled. "My sister, Kim, is a remarkable woman. If my mother were here, she'd be extraordinarily proud. The thing is, not just anyone could have talked me into being her man of honor, but she managed it. I'm still not sure how, but I think blackmail and tears were a part of the pitch." He paused as everyone laughed. "She's a warm, caring, good person. That's because of my parents. And then my dad's guiding hand after our mom died. They taught her to be honorable, courageous and loving.

"She was raised in this town where folks aren't just people who interact, but friends and neighbors." He let his gaze wander over everyone in the room. "So all of you are in some way, a good way, responsible for the amazing woman she is. I propose a toast to my sister, Kim, her new husband, Luke, God help him, my father and all of you who are the heart and soul of Blackwater Lake, where folks bring out the best in each other."

April listened to cheers and clapping as she looked at Will. He was relaxed and completely at home. Happy. Whether he realized it or not, he fit in here and his speech could reflect his subconscious desire to make a life in a place where folks brought out the best in each other. Was it possible he could be content in this small town instead of the big city? Content with her?

Against April's better judgment, hope sparked to life inside her. With luck it wouldn't bite her in the butt.

Chapter Thirteen

William knocked on April's sliding glass door with an elbow since his hands were full of flowers and wine. The sound wasn't loud, but she was in the kitchen and answered immediately.

"Hi." When she noticed the bouquet, there was a pleased, sort of soft expression in her eyes, the one he'd been hoping to see. "For me?"

"I think I made it clear at the wedding how I feel about carrying flowers. So they're definitely not for me." He handed over the cellophane-wrapped blooms.

"I love daisies. Baby's breath, and all the red and purple stuff in here I don't know the names of." She buried her nose in the blooms and sighed. "They're beautiful. Thank you, Will."

"You're welcome." When she tilted her face up he kissed her mouth softly.

"Come on in." She stepped back and let him by but

there was a puzzled expression on her face. "*Why* did you bring me flowers?"

"Because the bouquet Kim gave you is looking kind of—"

"Sad?" she finished for him.

"Yeah."

"Well, that's very sweet of you. Don't let the bad guys in Chicago know about this," she teased. "You'll lose tough-guy points in a big way."

"I'll take that risk." The happy look in her eyes was worth it.

He looked forward to seeing her every day after work and today was no exception. The wedding had been a couple of days ago, so the chaos was over and so was his excuse for coming to see her. The only one he had was that he wanted to.

"So why are you here?" she asked.

Will was beginning to wonder if she could read his mind. He was here because he liked her. She was beautiful, honest and never failed to call him on his crap. That was important and he wasn't even sure why. But she continued to look at him, waiting for an answer.

"I'm here hoping you'll take pity on me and feed me. Dad and Tim went out because there's no food in the house. Apparently Kim didn't shop the week before the wedding. Mani, pedi and hair appointments were more important than basic survival rations."

April stared at him. "Is that pouting? I think you're pouting."

"It's your imagination."

He stared right back at her and figured he got the better end of the deal. She was wearing khaki shorts and a spaghetti-strapped olive-green knit top that brought out the green in her eyes. Her sun-kissed brown hair was loose around her face and fell past her shoulders. God knew why he thought so, but her bare feet were so damn sexy. Probably should see a shrink about that because the feeling had nothing to do with sex. Okay, maybe a little. But mostly he got a sensation in his gut that drew him to her in a primitive, profound way.

"I don't believe you," she said, calling him on his crap. "The thing is, Kim is married now. She's going to live in her husband's house. Buy groceries for him. Someone across the alley is going to have to do the grocery shopping while she's on her honeymoon and Tim is too young. Not only does he not have a driver's license, which makes getting the stuff home a problem. But if he was turned loose, your dad would be on a steady diet of chips and Twinkies. Maybe an occasional candy bar with nuts in it just to get some protein. That's not the kind of food plan his doctor put him on."

"Dad's a big boy. He can shop."

"So can you." There was a sassy look in her eyes just for a second, then it disappeared.

Will knew the exact moment when she remembered he was leaving in about a week. He hated seeing the sunshine fade from her eyes. The thought of leaving her for good bothered him even more.

"You're right," he said. "I can shop."

She nodded and busied herself unwrapping the green cellophane from the flowers. Then she walked over to the cupboard. "I need a vase."

There was one on the top shelf, which she couldn't reach without a step stool. It was the place you put things not often used. Pretty soon what simmered between the two of them would be a top-shelf thing and it seemed like a colossal waste.

He moved behind her, close enough to feel the heat from her body without touching her. "I'll get that down for you."

"Thanks."

It was easy for him to reach up and carefully grab the crystal. "Here you go."

She took it from him and looked at the glass, a wistful, sad expression in her eyes. "This was my mother's."

"It's beautiful."

"I love it. Buying this was a splurge for her because there wasn't a lot of money for something that wasn't a necessity." April arranged the long stems in the vase and added water from the tap. "You know she always blamed herself for our splitting up."

"Why?"

"Because she got sick. I just couldn't go with you to Chicago."

"It wasn't her fault."

She nodded. "I could never quite convince her of that, though. Over and over I told her she was my mom. I couldn't be happy with you if I left her to face being sick alone. Someone had to help her fight the cancer."

"I know." That love and loyalty was one of the qualities he most admired in her. And if he'd waited...

This time with her in Blackwater Lake had been a do-over, a flash of what might have been. He'd screwed things up with her royally in the past, but she'd forgiven him. And these weeks of their fling were some of the happiest he could remember. In so many ways he felt like a new man.

She picked up the vase of flowers and put them on the kitchen table, which was already set for two. Meeting his gaze, she smiled. "It would please her to know I'm using the vase she loved enough to blow her budget on. Thanks again for bringing these, Will."

"You're welcome again." He pointed to the place settings on the table. "I see you were expecting me."

"Yeah. You've kind of gotten to be a habit." She shrugged.

"What are we having for dinner?" He sniffed. "Something smells really good."

"Oven-fried chicken, green salad, fruit." Her eyes sparkled. "And I stopped at Harvest Café and picked up two slices of strawberry cheesecake from their bakery case for dessert."

His empty stomach growled, but his heart was full. Part regret, part reluctance to leave her. When he'd agreed to her plan and a summer fling, it had felt like there was all the time in the world, but now it was nearly up.

A timer went off and she grabbed the potholder on a hook beside the microwave. After opening the bottom oven, she pulled out a cookie sheet filled with golden brown, sizzling chicken and placed it on the countertop to cool with a wire rack beneath.

"That looks as good as it smells. Better," he said.

She smiled. "I'll put everything on the table and we can eat."

"I'll open the wine. Apparently I'm channeling your culinary selections because it's a Chardonnay."

"Yum."

They worked together and in a few minutes took their usual seats at the table.

April moved the tall flowers aside. "I can't see you."

"Maybe that's not such a bad thing."

"I disagree." Her voice was quiet but the expression in her eyes said what she didn't put into words. She would miss him, too.

Will remembered what his dad had said about wanting to retire, but he couldn't or wouldn't unless Will took over the responsibilities of the job. But that wasn't the path he'd chosen for himself. No matter how much personal satisfaction he'd felt at making a difference here in Blackwater Lake, coming back meant failure to achieve a goal he'd worked very hard for. As long as he could remember, he'd wanted to be a Chicago PD detective. He'd had stars in his eyes about the job then, but after working it awhile, frustration set in that he couldn't catch the bad guys or get justice every time. Still…

He'd already failed at marriage. Failing in his career, too, made him a two-time loser. How was that anything to be proud of?

He poured some of her homemade oil-and-vinegar dressing on his salad, then mixed it in. Before he could stop himself, the words came out of his mouth. "Are you happy here in Blackwater Lake?"

Her fork stopped halfway to her mouth and her gaze lifted to his. "Why?"

"Just curious. I guess it was talking about your mom and staying here that triggered it." The thought had popped into his mind that she might have regrets about the path not taken. "I just…wondered."

She chewed a bite of salad, a thoughtful expression on her face. "My business is thriving and I really like what I do. People here are the best. If you need them, one phone call brings the posse. No questions asked. Family values are important to everyone. I love it here. There's nowhere else I'd rather be. I can't imagine living anywhere else."

He hadn't even realized he'd been holding his breath for a different answer until his bubble of expectation burst. "I'm glad for you."

She met his gaze. "I know you, Will. It surprises me sometimes how well I still do. I can tell by your expression that what I just told you isn't exactly what you wanted to hear."

"No, it wasn't." He'd been on the edge of asking her to go with him to Chicago. Again. Fortunately he kept those words to himself.

"You deserve all the best in life," he said, meaning that sincerely. "I'm happy that you have everything you want."

At least one of them did. She got under his skin and became a habit in the very best way possible.

But she was happy here and he couldn't ask her to leave.

He was going to have to break himself of her and it wasn't going to be easy.

"April, you're too good at this photography stuff," Lucy Bishop said. "I can't make up my mind between sunset over the lake or twilight on the mountain."

April smiled at her friend's praise. Business was slow at the Harvest Café this time of day and she'd dropped in to browse. "So when is your condo up on the mountain going to be ready for move-in?"

"They're starting to frame the building soon, so I'm being told six to nine months."

"But you're shopping now?"

"It makes me feel as if I'm making progress. Because, frankly, waiting for the first home I've ever purchased to be ready to move in to isn't going well."

"Patience is a virtue," April reminded her.

"Apparently not one that I have in abundance."

"At least you have a house to rent in the meantime. That's not easy to find."

"Yeah," Lucy said. "If Olivia Lawson hadn't fallen in love with Brady O'Keefe and moved in with him, I'd be homeless."

"Wow, Burke and Sloan Holden were onto something

when they decided to develop the land at the base of the mountain."

"I hear presales are through the roof," Lucy answered with a grin. "No pun intended."

April laughed. "Right."

After studying all the pictures again, she said, "I love this one with the sun just going down and the light painting the clouds pink, purple and gold."

"Shouldn't you wait to buy anything until you have a color scheme, not to mention a wall to hang it on?"

"Oh, I've chosen colors. Olive green, plum and rose."

"Sounds very feminine."

"What can I say? I enjoy being a girl. And I've been told that wall hangings don't need to fit in with the other colors of a room but should be something you love." She tapped her lip and gave the picture one more long, appraising look. "I'll take the sunset. It speaks to my soul."

"Thank you, Lucy. No one has ever paid me a nicer compliment." April gave her a hug. "Now it feels wrong to take your money."

"Oh, please—" Lucy waved her hand dismissively. "If I gave food away for free every time someone told me my meatloaf was a religious experience, Maggie and I would go broke. Then where would we be?"

"Well, she'd still be with Sloan Holden, but you wouldn't be able to pay your rent to Olivia," April said.

"Like I told you. Homeless," her friend agreed. "So, let that be a warning, missy. Don't give your work away."

"Roger that." April removed the picture from the wall and folded Bubble Wrap protectively around it. Then she rang up the sale and ran the credit card Lucy handed her. "So, what's new besides the condo?"

"That's code for am I dating anyone."

April laughed. "Are you?"

"No. And that's fine with me."

Come to think of it her friend hadn't been linked to any guy in Blackwater Lake since she'd arrived a few years ago. "I hear that writer comes into the café a lot."

"Jack Garner." Lucy looked thoughtful. "I wouldn't say a lot, but he comes in. Kind of keeps to himself. I respect that."

"You haven't flirted with him?" It was hard to believe this beautiful blue-eyed strawberry blonde was unattached.

"I flirt with everyone. It's called customer service. But he's a brooder. Good-looking, but trouble." Lucy's eyes narrowed. "Look at you peppering me with questions to distract me from asking what's up with you and Will Fletcher."

"I sincerely want to know what's going on with you." But April knew her protest was pointless since she'd been busted.

"And now you do." Her gaze turned curious. "So, you and Will. Details, my friend."

"*Friend* being the operative word… That's what Will and I are. Just friends. And when summer is over he's going back to Chicago to resume his detective job."

"The rumor is you two are really close. Are you getting serious?"

"No."

But last night April had gotten the feeling that he was thinking about asking her to go with him when he left. His question about whether or not she was happy in Blackwater Lake seemed more than idle chitchat. Talk about conflicted. To know that he felt more for her than casual friendship or a convenient hookup would have her doing the dance of joy. But if he'd actually asked her to go with him… Impossible choice.

When they were barely out of their teens, the decision had been easy. More than anything she'd wanted to be with Will. Now there was a whole lot more to consider. She had roots—a business, house and friends.

"But you're going to visit him in Chicago?" Lucy asked.

"I'm not planning to." She would never again risk finding him with a woman who was naked under his shirt. "Will and I have a past. A lot happened before you came to Blackwater Lake."

"I've heard."

Of course she had. "We tried the long-distance thing before and it didn't work out."

"Too bad." Lucy tsked. "You two are so cute together."

"We get that a lot."

They were a whole lot more than just cute together and she knew it by the way her heart squeezed painfully at the thought of him not being across the street at the sheriff's office. He spoke to her soul, April thought, and he had since she was sixteen years old. Soon they would have a public breakup and that would be that. This time she wasn't supposed to get hurt, but more and more that looked unlikely.

Lucy glanced at her watch, then picked up her purchase. "I have to get back to the café and supervise. The dinner rush starts about six and I've got an hour to get ready for it."

"Okay. Good to see you. Enjoy the picture."

"I plan to leave it wrapped. When I finally move, it will be like a surprise." Lucy waved on her way out the door.

April walked over to her big window that looked out on Main Street and the sheriff's office across the way. In a few more days Will would be gone and she would lose him for the second time. Technically she'd only had him once since this was simply a summer fling. Except tell that to her heart; this felt like more than a superficial flirtation.

She was restless, and business always dropped off around now because people were thinking about dinner. It couldn't hurt to close the shop a little early, so she put up the sign and locked the door. After looking both ways to make sure no cars were coming, she walked across the street and into the sheriff's office. Might not be the smartest thing she'd ever done, but soon she wouldn't be able to walk over and see him.

"Hey, April." Clarice's desk was a few feet inside the door. "Hope you're not here on business."

"No. Just wanted to stop in and say hi."

"Will's on the phone." Clarice obviously assumed, correctly, that he was the one she wanted to say hi to.

The door to his office was open and April could hear him talking and see him behind his desk. "How are you?" she said to the dispatcher.

"Great. Looking forward to end of summer and a little quiet time before tourists come in for ski season."

"Yeah."

"Been nice having Will here. When Hank got sick, I didn't know what we were going to do but Will sure stepped up."

"Yeah. It has been nice." She was going to miss him coming to her back door with pizza and wine. And nights without him in her bed were going to be lonely. Heck, just looking from her shop to the sheriff's office and knowing he wasn't here would be sad.

Then Will came out of his office and smiled when he saw her. He walked over and kissed her lightly on the lips. "This is a nice surprise."

"Glad you think so." She knew his behavior was part of the plan and when she was the one to give him the heave-ho, no one would pity her. Still, she felt the familiar flutter in her stomach that being around him always produced. "How's your day?"

"Let's just say the kids are ready for school to be back in."

"Bored?"

"Big time," he answered. "But I have to admit I'm a little on edge. Dad has his checkup with the doctor today for medical clearance to come back to work."

"Oh, Sheriff," Clarice said. "That reminds me. Buck Healy and Fred Turner are squabbling. Buck is coming in to fill out a formal complaint. But Eddie is out on patrol. Do you want me to dispatch him out there and save some paperwork?"

Will shook his head. "This needs a delicate touch. Those two have been bickering for years. If there was a God in heaven, they wouldn't share a property line, but they do. Somebody's cow, horse or goat probably ate someone's garden, grass or tractor. I'll go out and talk to them myself. It's easier if you know the history."

He sure did, April thought. The two feuding neighbors would listen to him because he was one of them, not an outsider. And, unlike Eddie, he was intimidating.

"Come on back to the office," he said to her.

"Don't you have to go and see Buck and Fred?"

"They'll keep for a few minutes."

"Okay." Her tummy did a happy little shimmy that he put off something for her.

She followed him into his office and he closed the door, then backed her against it. He pressed his body to hers. "I'm really, really glad you came in."

"Me, too." Her voice was a wanton whisper.

He lowered his head and touched his mouth to hers again, but this move was full of passion and promise, not meant for anyone else to see. His hands were braced on either side of her head and with his tongue he traced her mouth, urging it open. Her lips parted and he entered, sweeping inside with a groan. Their harsh breathing filled the office until another sound bled through it.

He pulled back, his eyes full of annoyance at the interruption. "Please tell me that's not my cell."

"Can't." She swallowed hard, not able to say much of anything at all.

"Damn." Reluctantly he moved away and walked over to his desk where his cell phone sat on a stack of files. He looked at the caller ID and there was an apologetic expression on his face. "I have to take this."

"No problem."

He hit a button and put the device to his ear. "Hey, Crash, how the heck are you?" After listening he said, "Sorry to hear things are falling apart without me."

Obviously the person on the other end was his detective partner from Chicago. It had been easy to pretend that life didn't exist for him until now, but this reminder tightened a knot in her stomach.

April drew in a deep breath and with a gesture asked if he wanted her to step out while he talked. Will shook his head and leaned a hip on the corner of his desk. She sat in one of the chairs in front of it.

"Things here?" Will asked. "This is a sleepy little town where littering the sidewalk is major crime."

That was just the way April liked it, but he sounded bored. Work in Chicago no doubt was more exciting than spiteful, decidedly *un*neighborly neighbors. But excitement wasn't all it was cracked up to be. Some things were more important. Except she knew him pretty well and he'd always craved excitement. Same old, same old day after day didn't thrill him.

"Hang in there, my friend." Will grinned at whatever his partner said. "Don't worry. It's not that much longer until I'll be back to bail you out. Just a couple more days." He listened and nodded. "Yeah, after Labor Day."

And from the tone in his voice it sounded as if that couldn't be a moment too soon for him. Obviously he couldn't wait to return to his job. It was also obvious by the pain in April's heart that she'd hoped he wanted to be with her enough to stay.

She'd fallen in love with him again. Or, more precisely, she'd never fallen out of love. He'd asked her the night before if she was happy here in Blackwater Lake. She'd said she had everything right here.

But that wasn't exactly true.

She didn't have everything she wanted because she couldn't have Will.

Chapter Fourteen

April paced her kitchen, waiting for news on Hank. He'd seen the doctor that day to determine whether or not he could return to work. And here was another classic conflict. She sincerely hoped the man got a clean bill of health and could go back to doing whatever he wanted to do—being sheriff or running a marathon. Although that would be a miracle since, to her knowledge, he'd never run one before. She loved him like a father and wished him all the best.

On the other hand it would also give Will the green light to leave town. Not that he could stick around indefinitely, but a little longer would be nice. He wouldn't stay for her, but he might for his dad.

She'd been home from work for a while now and if someone didn't tell her something soon…

Just then there was a knock on the sliding glass door and she saw Will standing there. Thank God.

After hurrying over she unlocked and opened it. "What's the verdict? How is he?"

"The doc said he's doing great. He's in arguably the best shape of his life. Returning to work is not a problem." There was an odd look on Will's face.

"What's wrong?"

"Nothing." He forced a smile. "It's great news."

"It certainly is." She forced cheerfulness into her voice and felt as slimy as polluted water for not feeling 100 percent happy. "He gave us quite a scare and it's wonderful how he completely turned everything around."

"Yet another way my father leads by example."

"Your father is a truly amazing man who is admired by all. I'm so lucky to live across the alley from him."

Or unlucky, one could argue.

If she'd never met Will, her heart might not have been broken even once, let alone twice by the same man. Someday she might embrace the sentiment that it was better to have loved and lost than to never have loved at all. But today was not that day.

"He's a good neighbor," Will agreed.

"He's a good man," she said again, mostly because she didn't want to say anything about their next step.

"Yeah." He dragged his fingers through his hair. "If we keep this up, he should qualify for sainthood pretty soon."

"I guess." What they were doing was called procrastination, putting off what they really needed to talk about. And that was just fine with her. "He must be looking forward to getting back to work."

"I suppose."

"He hasn't said?" That surprised her and actually wasn't really an answer. She got the feeling there was something he wasn't telling her. "Well, I'm sure folks will be glad to have him back. Not that you aren't doing a great job, Will. I didn't mean to imply you weren't. It's just that everyone wants normal, whatever that is. And normal is him wearing the badge. And for you to…not." She shrugged. "I'm babbling."

"Really?" His smile didn't quite make it to his eyes. "I didn't notice."

"Some detective you are," she said wryly.

She could banter with him all night and maybe that would squash the pain that was scratching to get out. From experience she knew how bad it would be when that happened.

Unfortunately when she said the word *detective*, that burst the protective bubble they were both working to keep inflated. Regret settled in his eyes and there was tension in his jaw. The Band-Aid was getting ripped off, ready or not.

"April…"

She turned away. "All joking aside, Will, this really is good news. It's also your cue to go back to Chicago."

"Yeah, it is."

"Your partner will be glad to have you back." She took a deep breath and faced him again. "I couldn't help overhearing your end of the conversation earlier in your office."

"So you *were* eavesdropping."

"You told me to stay." She shrugged.

"I know. And, yeah, Pete seemed ready to have me back."

"You must be beyond ready to go back," she said, sort of hoping he would say she was wrong about that.

"Like you said. Normal. Chicago is that for me." He was wearing his law-enforcement face, the one that didn't let on what was going through his mind. The one he'd probably perfected during criminal interrogations.

"Normal is good. I'm a strong advocate of normal."

"It's time to implement the final part of the plan," he gently reminded her.

If everything had gone according to the plan Kim had

suggested, April wouldn't feel like this. Her job was to get him to fall in love with her, then publicly dump him. It wasn't part of her agenda to be the only one falling in love. So, when had things gone so horribly wrong?

Okay, she told herself, grow a spine. The endgame was to put herself back in the driver's seat and not be pitied because Will Fletcher got away again. Growing a spine started here and now.

She met his gaze and put as much spunk into hers as possible. "So, before we take the end of this fling public, I have to ask. You didn't fall for me at all?"

He looked away for a moment, then said, "That isn't the way you pitched me the plan."

Something told her that was all the answer she was going to get. "Any idea how to pull off the final scene of our charade?"

"Actually, I do." He folded his arms over his chest.

Maybe it was hope on her part, but she thought that pose might be to keep from touching her because he didn't trust himself to do that and no more. Maybe she was a little irresistible to him. Without a doubt she knew if he put his hands on her she'd be lost.

"So, you have thoughts. Care to share?"

"There's a spur-of-the-moment celebration of Dad's good news and it will be at the Grizzly Bear Diner."

"I wonder if his heart doctor would approve of him having a hamburger," she mused.

"I believe he's a salad convert even though my sister isn't around to be the food police. She's still on her honeymoon," he added.

"Right. So when is this get-together taking place?" she asked.

"Now. The mayor will be there. The town council. All

the Blackwater Lake movers and shakers. Word is spreading and I'm sure there will be a lot of people."

"In other words it will be gossip central."

"Right." His eyes went blank, grew darker. His cop face. "It should get the job done. I'm thinking it will work better if we walk in together and break the news."

"Okay."

"You say whatever you want to. Although I'd appreciate it if you didn't make me out to be too big a jerk."

She smiled and did her best to keep sadness out of it. "We've already established that I'm not a good liar, so staying close to the truth is best. And the truth is you're not a jerk."

"Thanks for that." He nodded resolutely. "I'll just follow your lead."

"Okay, then."

He moved close and curved his fingers around her upper arms then hesitated before kissing her forehead. "Let's do this."

Let's not, she thought, although it was obvious he'd just said goodbye.

Thirty minutes later they walked into the Grizzly Bear Diner, which was filled to overflowing. The crowd was probably beyond capacity, but no one seemed inclined to enforce any ordinances on an occasion like this.

People parted for them as they made their way to a booth in the center of the establishment where Tim sat with a friend while his grandfather stood and shook hands. Hank was generally soaking up congratulations and good wishes.

April really hated to rain on his parade, but this venue was better than the Labor Day parade to get the word out. Everyone was under one roof and this news would spread like the flu virus. She just needed an opening, then would make it as quick and painless as possible.

Hank grinned when he saw them and opened his arms to hug her. "Glad you two finally showed up."

"Sorry." She stepped away from him and rubbed the side of her nose. "Will and I had some things to discuss."

The older man frowned. "What's wrong?"

And there was her opening. "First I want to say how happy I am that you have medical clearance to return to work."

A cheer erupted around her proving that not only did her words carry, but people were listening. She wondered if there would be any sound to hear when her heart cracked.

When everyone quieted down, Hank said, "What else do you have on your mind? Something's bothering you, April."

All of a sudden she got cold feet. This was his party, a celebration of his hard work to get back up and running. This grand gesture was all about her, so she should be the one to decide whether or not to do it. "It's okay. I'll tell you later."

Hank shook his head. "Maybe I can help. You'll feel better if you get it off your chest."

Usually when she unburdened herself to this man she did feel better, but that wasn't going to happen with this news. "It can wait."

"No. The doctor says I need to keep stress to a minimum. And now you've got me worried. So spill it."

Oh, brother, she'd really stepped in it and had no choice. *Quick and simple*, she told herself. "The thing is, I called it quits with Will tonight."

Hank studied her as a whisper started through the crowd. "I see. Why is that?"

"He's not the right man for me." Keep it simple like he'd

said, she thought. Make it all about her and don't embellish. "We had fun this summer, but that's all it would ever be with us. I want more. And he doesn't define 'more' the same way I do."

The father looked at his son and there was no mistaking the disappointment in his eyes. "That true, Will?"

"Yes. She's a remarkable woman and deserves a man who can make her happy. Someone who won't hurt her."

"I'm the one walking away." She raised her voice, making it determined, definite. No one should doubt that she was in control even though it didn't feel that way. "It's what I want and that makes it best for both of us."

It was quiet enough to hear a pin drop, which was unusual for the diner, then everyone around them started whispering.

Hank was silent for a moment before reluctantly nodding. He cupped her cheek in a big hand. "I guess you know best, honey."

"Thanks for understanding," she said. Wow, she'd never anticipated the effort it would take not to cry. But tears would dilute the effect of what she was trying to accomplish.

At least fate was on her side a little bit because at that moment one of the servers brought a pitcher of beer and some glasses. "Chicken wings and nachos are coming. And a salad for you, Sheriff," he said.

April gave Will one last look and nodded him a thank-you as she backed away. Right now she was numb to the murmurs of sympathy directed at her as she slowly moved toward the diner's exit. She tried to be proud of herself, but this didn't feel at all like the win Kim had promised when hatching this plan.

Lucy Bishop was standing in the waiting area by the front door. "April, I just heard."

"What?" Could news of the breakup really have spread that fast?

"You dumped Will Fletcher." Sympathy welled up in her eyes. "I'm sorry things didn't work out for you two."

News *had* traveled that fast. "I didn't want to give him false hope."

"You're really strong. And wise."

April waited to feel some satisfaction but there wasn't any to be had what with her heart breaking. The only win was that in Blackwater Lake she would no longer be that poor girl Will Fletcher left behind.

April took the fresh batch of her healthy whole-wheat macaroni and low-fat cheese out of the oven and set it on a warming tray. Cooking was her desperate attempt to fill the void Will had left in her life when he went back to Chicago a week ago. So far cooking wasn't helping all that much. And she wasn't eating much of it. Mostly the food was going across the alley to Hank Fletcher. Hence the health-conscious alterations.

He was lonely, too.

Will had only been back in her life for the summer, but she missed him terribly and felt more alone than she ever had in her life. But her neighbor had seen his daughter married, then stood by while she and her son moved out of his house and in with her husband, where they would start their new life as a family. Hank had supported April through so many changes, good and bad, so she planned to return the favor. This time they could help each other.

She got out her casserole carrier and food warmer, then slid the dish inside before letting herself out the kitchen's sliding glass door. It was hard not to picture Will here, not to remember the first time he'd stood there looking completely adorable holding a pizza box and bottle of wine.

Hard to forget every moment with him after that night. There were memories everywhere she turned and each one was like a blow to her soul.

Tears filled her eyes as she walked across the alley to Hank's house. Lights were on inside that indicated he was home from work so she knocked.

The door opened and Hank stood there in suit pants, a white dress shirt and snappy red tie. "Hi, kiddo."

Looking past him she saw a matching suit jacket slung over one of the kitchen chairs. "Are you going out?"

"I'm taking Josie to Fireside for dinner," he explained. "I wanted to thank her for being there for Kim when I went to the hospital."

"Is it more than a thank-you?"

"Maybe." He opened the door wider. "Come on in."

She hesitated. "I don't want to make you late."

"Don't worry about it." He indicated the dish in her hands. "I guess that's for me."

"Yeah. But obviously you don't need it."

"If it's good warmed up, I need it," he said.

"All right, then." She handed it over and walked inside.

"Thanks, honey." He took the dish, then frowned at her when their gazes met. "What's wrong?"

"Nothing. I'm fine."

"The hell you are." He set the macaroni and cheese on the island, then took her elbow and guided her to the kitchen table where he sat her in a chair. "You're going to tell me all about what's bothering you."

"But you have a d-date." Then the sobs started and she felt horrible because she was really happy for him. Dating was a good thing.

He pulled one of the other chairs closer and sat in front of her. "It can wait. But you need to talk to me, April. I can see how unhappy you are. Hell, you've been unhappy since that night at the diner. You said breaking up with Will would be the best thing, but I'm not seeing it."

She drew in a shuddering breath and brushed tears from her cheeks. "Gosh, and here I thought I'd been hiding it pretty well."

"You don't have to do that with me, honey." There was sympathy in his eyes. Will's eyes. "And it's pointless to try. I can see through you. Always could."

"Good to know." She sniffled.

"This is about Will." It wasn't a question.

"Since I can't hide anything from you... Yeah," she admitted. "This is about Will. I really miss him."

"Me, too."

"This is so stupid. *I'm* so stupid." She shook her head. "Here I am feeling sorry for myself when you've suddenly got an empty nest."

She looked at him, really looked. He was still a handsome man who had the passage of time stamped on his face and silver in his hair. This is what his son would look like, but she wouldn't be there beside Will to share the good and bad things that left a mark on a life. The realization made her deeply and profoundly sad.

"Look, April, I love my family. You know that. But—" He stopped and listened for a few moments. "Do you hear that?"

"No. What?"

"It's called quiet. That's the absence of noise. And there's something else."

April glanced around the kitchen and tried to figure out what he meant. But she had no idea what he was talking about. "I don't feel anything."

"The energy level is as it should be."

"I don't understand."

"Because you're young." He sighed. "It's like this. A

man of my age likes his peace and quiet. Some would call it boring. I prefer to think of it as tranquility."

"Okay," she said hesitantly.

"Do I miss them?" He shrugged. "I would if they moved halfway around the world, but right now not so much. If I need a dose of chaos, I can pick up the phone and see if it's okay to drop by their house. Then I come back here to chill out."

"Or go out. With Josie," she teased.

"That, too." He grinned. "Don't get me wrong. I wouldn't trade the experience of having my daughter here and getting to know my grandson so well. I would do anything for them. But I'm fine being by myself."

"I'm glad."

"But you're not. Fine, I mean." He took her hand in his big warm ones. "Just so you know, I'm aware of the little scheme Kim came up with to get you and Will together."

"How?"

"Not much happens in this town that I don't know about. I heard things and put two and two together. Then she confessed everything when she got back from the honeymoon and heard he left town."

His words finally sank in. "Wait, she was pushing Will and me together? She claimed it was about closure for me. So I could move on." And it all worked out so well, she thought.

"Yeah, that was her cover story. But she was matchmaking. You and Will are pretty stubborn—"

"Will might be." After all they'd been to each other he still left. "But not me," she protested.

"Right." He smiled and apparently decided not to argue that point. "Anyway, she felt strongly that if you two gave it another chance, you'd see that you belong together. That's why she talked you into making him fall for you. It meant you'd have to spend time with him and rekindle what you had before. But she didn't expect that you would actually dump him."

"If you suspected, why didn't you tip Will off to what was going on?" Although she remembered when she confessed the ruse, Will had said he suspected something was up. Like father, like son.

"I thought this whole conspiracy had a decent shot at succeeding," Hank admitted. "And I wouldn't mind you and Will together. I'd have liked that very much."

"Me, too." Unexpectedly she smiled. "But your approval means a lot to me. Even if there's no Will and me to approve of."

"Of course I approve. You're a very special woman. Not like that one he married. I never liked her."

"Neither did Kim." She would have to conclude that was a family thing.

"I know." Hank looked down for a moment, then met her gaze. "My kids think I'm not observant, but they'd be wrong. I just pick and choose what I say and when I say it."

"Probably smart."

"I'm a cop and have been for a lot of years. Details are important and I don't miss them."

"I've always suspected that about you," she said.

He gave her a small smile. "I'm not blowing my own horn here, just stating facts. And I have a point."

"Which is?"

"From the time you turned sixteen years old I've seen the way my son looks at you, April. He's loved you since then and I don't think he's ever stopped."

"Then why did he go—?" Her voice cracked and she caught her bottom lip between her teeth.

"Some misguided sense of honor. The boy knows I want to retire and that the job is his if he wants it."

"I wasn't aware. Will never told me the sheriff's job could be his."

"I've always taught him and his sister to finish what they start. The lesson took real well with him. He's got this thing in his head that leaving Chicago is something to be ashamed of on top of his marriage not working out."

"I see. Then it's really up to him, isn't it?" She nodded sadly. "Thanks for telling me this, Hank."

"I thought you should know." He stood up and folded his arms over his chest. "You're like a daughter to me and I want the best for you."

"That really means a lot."

"And this has to be said. Will is my son. I love him and mostly I'm proud of him." He shook his head in exasperation. "But when it comes to romantic relationships he's not the sharpest knife in the drawer."

"He loves his career and I love mine. We just aren't meant to be." She smiled sadly. "I guess we are both stubborn. Neither of us would bend."

"He just can't see what's in front of him, what's good for him," Hank said. "And it's not easy for a father to watch and not say anything, to let him figure it out for himself. Sometimes you have to walk around with duct tape over your mouth. Metaphorically speaking."

"Well, you're a wise man, Hank Fletcher. And I'm glad that you know I didn't really mean it when I said he's not the man for me. The thing is, he never asked me to go with him…" She lifted her shoulders in a shrug. "On the bright side, at least no one in town pities me this time."

"I didn't pity you last time," Hank said. "It's Will I feel sorry for. I think that job in Chicago is sucking the life out of him and there's nothing I can do. I was hoping you could talk him out of going back."

"I didn't try. If I had, he would only resent me and that

would ultimately destroy us. He had to want to be with me enough and—" she shrugged "—he didn't."

"I know it. Don't like it," he added, "but I know it's true."

April stood and hugged him. "Thank you for listening to me whine."

"Didn't sound like complaining to me, but anytime you need to talk, I'm here for you, honey." He gave her a good squeeze, then stepped back. "You're not alone, you know that. I'm always here for you. You might not be family by blood, but you are by choice and heart. Sometimes that bond is even stronger."

Tears gathered in her eyes again, but this time she smiled. "I'm so lucky to have you."

"I'm the lucky one."

"It's possible you'll get even luckier tonight," she teased. "Say hi to Josie for me."

"Will do."

April left and walked across the dark alley, letting the tears roll down her cheeks unchecked. There was no one to see now. No one to put on a front for. The good news was that she hadn't lost the family who'd taken her under its wing so many years ago.

The bad news was that she was finding out that losing Will for the second time was twice as painful.

Chapter Fifteen

Will looked around the Chicago squad room of the Twelfth Precinct. There were rows of desks with phones, files and computers. The walls had multiple bulletin boards with wanted posters and notices. Activity and excitement hummed in the air. He waited to feel excited about being back, but there was nothing. Since he'd returned a couple weeks ago, he figured the feeling probably wasn't going to happen. There were no windows and even if he could look out one, he would see brick buildings and dingy storefronts in this area of the city. No mountains and clear, blue sky.

Everyone had greeted him with assurances that he'd been missed and there were case files stacked up on his desk to prove it. If all went well, one of them would be closing in a little while.

He'd received an anonymous tip about a drug deal going down and it had turned out to be reliable. He and Pete had made three arrests and the perps were cooling their heels in holding. That would soften them up for interrogation.

During the takedown a crowd had gathered. That always happened, but this time there was something different. As he was cuffing a kid only a little older than his nephew, there'd been a woman in his peripheral vision. His heart had jolted as if he'd been smacked in the chest. For a split second he'd thought she was April. And in that second his emotions ran the gamut from pure exhilaration that she'd changed her mind and followed him to fear for her safety in a fluid and dangerous situation.

His concentration slipped and the kid obviously felt it because he'd twisted away and run. Will chased him and easily brought the kid down. In a slimy puddle. His jeans and T-shirt were never going to be the same. Even worse, the woman wasn't April.

"Welcome back to the Twelfth," he muttered to himself.

Pete Karlik walked over and sat at his desk that faced Will's. "They just brought the drug seller up from holding. He's in interrogation room one."

"Okay."

Pete's sharp blue eyes narrowed. "Something bugging you?"

"Nope."

His partner was thirty-five years old, smart and built like a bull. He'd been married to his high school sweetheart for fourteen years and they had two kids—a boy who was thirteen and a ten-year-old girl. As far as anyone here at the precinct knew the guy had never cheated on his wife. Chicago born and bred, Pete was a good cop who loved his city and would do anything to keep it safe. Dedication like that was something special, something reserved for a hometown boy.

After studying Will for several moments, he nodded. "So, how do you want to handle this? We both know this kid is a low-level flunky. He's expendable to them but could give us information, names, to bring down the organization. Or at least put cracks in it. If we can get him to crack."

"Good cop, bad cop?" Will suggested. He'd played both roles and so had Pete.

The other man looked doubtful. "He's young, but I'd bet the farm he doesn't scare easy. He's hanging out with some really bad guys."

"Okay. You don't think we can rattle him." Will thought for a moment. "We can lay out his options. Reality check."

"Maybe." His partner mulled that over. "If we can imply that the other two scumbags are rolling on him, it could give us leverage to make him see the light."

Will nodded. "Only one of them gets a deal and that would be the first one who talks."

"Okay. Let's work it that way." Pete pushed his desk chair back to stand up when his phone rang. "Karlik." He listened and the frown on his face said there wasn't going to be meaningful information forthcoming from the perp. "Okay, Sarge. Thanks. You just saved us a trip up there."

After his friend disconnected from the call Will said, "He lawyered up."

"Yeah." Pete's expression grew darker. "You're good, Fletcher. Keep it up and you might just make detective someday."

"You're a funny guy." But this situation wasn't the least bit funny. "So much for taking down the big boys."

"Sometimes I wonder why we bother." Pete pounded a fist on his desk. "Do you ever feel like you're one step behind the bad guys?"

Will folded his arms over his chest. "Try five steps."

"And we'll never catch up."

He'd never heard his friend so pessimistic. "Since when did you turn into a glass-half-empty kind of guy?"

"Mine's not half-empty," Pete said. "I don't even have a glass."

This wasn't like the "Crash" Karlik Will knew. He suspected whatever was causing it was bigger than the job. "What's bugging *you*, pard?"

"It's Ryan." The man rubbed a hand over his face. "He was at a party that was raided by the cops. They found drugs. A lot. Regular pharmacies should be so well stocked. Street stuff there, too. The guys who answered the call knew me and gave me a heads-up. Abbie and I decided to let them bring him into the precinct and scare the crap out of him."

"Geez, man." Will's closest experience to having kids was his nephew. They'd had a very short discussion about girls and birth control. He felt guilty for not being more a part of the boy's life. But if Tim had been arrested at a party where illegal substances were found, he'd probably freak. And there was one question he'd ask. "Did Ryan use?"

Pete met his gaze, worry stark in his own. "He swears he didn't. His mother and I tend to believe him. Yeah, I know all parents say this, but he's a good kid."

"Of course he is. You and Abbie raised him."

"I don't want to stick my head in the sand either. If he's got a problem we need to know so we can help him."

"Yeah."

Will thought about the teens he'd busted in Blackwater Lake for spray painting structures and egging cars. Neither of them had asked for a lawyer and didn't know to do it because they'd never been in serious trouble. Things didn't get complicated with arrests and paperwork. He'd been in front of the situation and made a real, positive difference. It felt good.

"He's grounded now and we have to go to court. If the

judge wants to throw the book at him we're okay with that. Scare the hell out of him. It's a juvenile record and can be erased. He can learn from this and with luck it will be a cheap lesson."

"Sounds like a good plan," Will agreed.

Pete sighed. "But what if he doesn't learn? What if he goes to another party when he's not grounded and there are drugs? He was at a friend's house this time. Someone we know and thought was okay. These are the kids he's hanging out with. What if—"

"Those two words will make you crazy, man." Will held up a hand. "Don't go there."

"I wish it was that easy."

"Look, you shouldn't listen to me." Will blew out a long breath. "I don't have kids."

"Why is that?"

"What?"

"Why don't you have kids?" Pete asked.

"Because I married the wrong woman."

"Yeah, you did, buddy. I never liked her. No offense."

"None taken. My dad and sister said the same thing." Will laughed. "It seems to be the prevailing sentiment."

"How's your dad doing?"

"Great." Will missed him. He'd enjoyed having coffee in the morning, discussing things that happened on the job with the man who knew the challenges better than anyone. The man who'd offered the job to him.

"Must have been nice to spend some time with the family," Pete said.

"It was." And April.

Just thinking about her made him smile. Then the emptiness inside him opened wider because he couldn't walk across the alley and knock on her sliding glass door. He couldn't watch her beautiful face light up with pleasure at the exact moment she recognized him. There wasn't going to be an "accidental" meeting outside their back doors that would result in a run together.

He missed her so damn much.

"What's her name?" Pete asked.

"Who?"

"The one you left behind. The one who should have been your baby mama?"

Will knew better than to blow off the question. This man had taught him a lot about interviewing people and could see right through him. "Her name is April. What gave me away?"

"Besides the fact that you say her name as if you're in church?" Pete shrugged, the gesture saying it was easy to figure out. "And you've been different since you got back. It's not job burnout. I know that when I see it. But your heart's not in it anymore. You had the fire in the belly when you first got here, but it went out a long time ago." Pete thought about what he'd just said. "It's like your heart is somewhere else entirely."

"Someday you're going to have to tell me how you get into my head like that."

"No big secret, man. You let that kid slip away today. That's not like you. I just knew you were thinking about her." He grinned. "April. Like spring."

"Yeah."

"And I'll tell you something else, Will. Remember it's worth what you paid for it." Pete leaned forward and rested his forearms on the desk. "I vent about stuff, but I wouldn't change it. Chicago is in my blood. Abbie's, too. We'll raise our family here and the kids will be fine. But your heart isn't here anymore. You need to be where you left it."

"But—"

"No *buts*." Pete pointed a finger at him, all Chicago attitude. "That's not a career failure. It's a choice. There's a difference."

Will's life flashed before his eyes, but it had nothing to do with near-death experience. This city was big and there were parts that were like nowhere else. Beautiful parts. But it was also crowded, noisy, dirty. And most of all April wasn't here. Pete was right. He had a choice.

"You know," his partner said, "while you were gone the captain had me partnered with Jimmy Gutierrez. He's a good cop and has a lot to learn. Reminds me of you."

Will nodded. He got what his friend was saying and pulled out his cell phone, then speed-dialed his sister. The call went straight to voice mail, but he left a message.

"Kim, I need you to do something for me."

April let Kim drag her from the parking lot just inside Blackwater Lake town limits to the sidewalk on Main Street. Come hell or high water they were going to the farmer's market and her friend wouldn't take no for an answer. April wasn't very happy about it, but she wasn't happy about much these days.

"I could have slept in today," she complained as her friend tugged her along.

"Not if you want to get the freshest fruits and vegetables."

"I don't. Old and stale is fine with me." When Will left, he had taken with him all the color in her life. These days her world was black-and-white.

"Old and stale isn't healthy." Kim pointed to the crowd assembled a distance away at the end of the street where it was blocked off. "Look at all those people. They're taking the fresh food right out of your mouth."

"I'm okay with that. Hey, slow down," she protested when her friend linked arms and increased the pace.

"The good stuff is going fast."

"You should have come by yourself. I'm just slowing you down."

"I didn't want to come by myself. I wanted you here." There was an edge of aggravation to Kim's voice, but she seemed determined to project cheerful, friendly enthusiasm.

"What's wrong with you?"

"I'm sure I don't know what you mean."

April looked sideways, wondering who this woman was and what she'd done with Kim. "When did you start talking like Scarlett O'Hara?"

"Well, fiddledeedee." She grinned then drew in a deep breath. "Isn't it a beautiful day for a—" She stopped and for just a moment there was a horrified expression on her face.

"For what? Kim, what the heck is going on with you today? Seriously, you're acting a little weird."

"Nothing. It's just a beautiful day to go to the farmer's market with my best friend. I've been busy with back-to-school stuff, and settling Tim and me into family life. You and I haven't had a chance to really talk since before I got married. Sensational pictures, by the way. Luke and I are still trying to make up our minds which ones to order for the album."

"Take your time." April felt a little guilty about being such a grump.

Black-and-white was a very narrow palette. She sighed and tamped down the tiny bit of envy that wouldn't go away. Just because Kim had gotten everything she'd ever wanted and April had lost the love of her life for the second time, that was no reason to compromise a beautiful friendship. She chalked it up to a very human flaw and resolved to work on it.

"How is married life?" she asked.

"Pretty great." Kim positively glowed. "I like being a Mrs. It's nice to have someone to count on. Oh, I know my family is there, but this is different."

"I'm really happy for you." April filled the words with a lot of phony eagerness and topped it off with a big, fake smile.

"No, you're not." Kim scoffed. "And I don't blame you. It's hard being this happy when my best friend in the whole world is miserable. I can't believe my brother is so stupid."

"Yeah. About that… Your dad told me your plan," she put air quotes around the word, "was nothing more than an attempt at matchmaking."

"Nobody's perfect." Kim shrugged. "I was so sure it would work. I'm so very sorry he hurt you, sweetie."

"You meant well." As they continued walking, April leaned her head on her friend's shoulder for just a moment. "Not your fault Will didn't cooperate."

"He'll come around. You watch. And I'll bet you twenty bucks that he'll be back." There was such confidence in her voice.

"I'll take that bet." April wanted to be a believer, but it was too hard to be wrong. "Because I'm not going to live in False Hope–ville anymore. That painful episode is behind me."

They were passing the Harvest Café where Lucy Bishop had just walked out the door. She smiled. "Hey, you two. How's it going?"

"Good," Kim said. "We're on our way to the farmer's market."

"Me, too. Mind if I join you?"

"That would be great." Kim sounded too eager, almost relieved to have company.

"I go every week, but I'm running late today," Lucy

shared. "I like to beat the crowd and pick out the best fruits and veggies for the café." She glanced up the street. "This is the most crowded time to go."

"True," Kim agreed. "Most of the town will be there now."

"How are you holding up?" Lucy said to April. "I mean with Will gone?"

She heard the pity in her friend's voice. So much for the brilliant plan to change that. It had been too much to expect that if she broke up with him she'd no longer be the girl he left behind. Because he went to Chicago and she was still here, that made her—wait for it—the girl he left behind *again*.

"I'm great," April said. "Just peachy. At least, I will be."

"Good for you," Lucy said.

They were now a block away from their target destination. In the cordoned-off street there were several big blue tarps set up. Beneath them were tables holding crates filled with seasonal fresh produce. Lettuce, zucchini, squash, mushrooms and carrots. Beside them apples, pears and yams were displayed. The crowd was so thick you had to wait your turn to even get close to the bins.

The three of them stopped just outside the first tarp and listened to the hum of voices. The closest people to her waved, said hello and gave her pitying looks. She was just about to turn around and go back the way she'd come when Hank Fletcher walked over with Josie Swanson.

The trim older woman had big blue eyes and a warm smile. Her silver hair was cut in a flattering pixie style. "Hi, April. Haven't seen you for a while."

"How are you, Josie?"

"Great. If you don't factor in that I'll be homeless soon."

"Is Maggie Potter kicking you out?" April asked. The older woman was a widow and rented a room from the recently engaged single mom who'd fallen in love with Sloan Holden.

"Maggie would never do that," Josie said. "It's my decision. Young couples need their privacy."

Hank put his arm across her shoulders. "She's teasing. Actually she's moving in with me. I'm renting out Kim's old room." He winked at his daughter, a sign that he knew he wasn't fooling her with that story.

"You don't waste any time, Dad. My bed is hardly cold."

April knew her friend approved of the relationship. Josie had been there for the family during Hank's health crisis, and his daughter liked her very much. She sighed. Another happy couple.

As they waited their turn to walk under the tarp, the five of them talked, their voices raised against the backdrop of buzzing chatter all around them. April realized it was slowly quieting and finally stopped just as the crowd parted to let a man through.

It was a man who looked an awful lot like Will!

He walked right up to her. "I'm not okay with you dumping me."

Surely a heart couldn't beat as fast as hers was without some kind of consequence. "I thought you were in Chicago."

"I came back. For good," he added.

"I don't understand. What are you doing *here*?" Why hadn't he walked across the alley and knocked on her sliding glass door to tell her this?

"You broke up with me in public and I need to get you back the same way." There was a mother lode of determination in his blue eyes. "Besides, I have a better chance here with the whole town on my side."

"But how did you know I'd be here?" April glanced at Kim, who was looking awfully self-satisfied. Then it hit her. Why her friend had wheedled and bullied her into coming. "You forced me into this. You knew he'd be here."

"Actually he ordered me to get you here," Kim clarified. "And when the sheriff of Blackwater Lake gives you a direct order, it's always best to do what he says."

April thanked her friend with a look that she knew would be understood. "So when you bet me twenty bucks he'd be back—"

Kim shrugged. "Sucker bet."

"I'm not paying you," she vowed. "You should have warned me he would be here—"

"I told her not to tell you. I was afraid if you knew, you wouldn't come," Will said. "And I really wanted— no, needed—you to."

"Why?" Wariness warred with hope inside her. She was stunned and shocked and so darn happy to see him.

"I thought a career in a big-city police department was running *to* something, but I was wrong. Everything in the world that's important to me is right here. I wanted to ask you to come with me when I left, but you're so happy here." His gaze never left hers and his eyes were filled with intensity. "The thing is, you're the smart one. You stayed. But I finally wised up and came back. Not just for you, but this town. It gets into your blood in the best possible way."

"That it does," she said.

"And you got into my blood. You stole my heart when you were sixteen years old and you have it now."

April actually heard a collective sigh from the women in the crowd. "I don't know what to say."

"A simple yes would be just about perfect," he said, his voice low and deep. "Because I love you, April. And I'd really like it if you'd marry me."

Before his words even sank in everyone gathered around them started chanting, "Yes! Yes! Yes!"

How could she say no when he was offering her everything she'd ever wanted in her life? She needed no encouragement from the crowd and threw herself into his arms, then said for all to hear, "Yes!"

"And we got an affirmative." That was Hank's voice and the words incited applause and cheers.

She smiled up at the man she'd loved for as long as she could remember. "Sounds like your dad approves."

"I'm glad. But it wouldn't matter if he didn't. I can be a bonehead sometimes, but of course you know that better than anyone. On the upside, I don't very often make the same mistake twice."

"No you don't," she agreed. "Kim was right. I've never stopped loving you."

"I told you everything would work out." Kim sniffled loudly. "Happy endings always make me cry."

April had just about given up on living happily ever after but this was definitely worth waiting for. She gave Will a sassy look. "Does this mean I get to be your side-kick?"

"For as long as we live," he promised.

She would never have guessed it was possible to be this happy and wished her mother was there to share in it. But she had a strong feeling that her mom was smiling down on them. And just maybe had a hand in making her dream of a family with Will come true.

April was no longer the girl he'd left behind, but the one he'd come home to.

* * * * *

SPECIAL EXCERPT FROM

 HARLEQUIN®

SPECIAL EDITION

*Zoe Robinson refuses to believe she's a secret Fortune,
but she can't deny the truth—she's falling for
Joaquin Mendoza! But can this Prince Charming
convince his Cinderella to find happily-ever-after with
him once he uncovers his own family secrets?*

Read on for a sneak preview of
FORTUNE'S PRINCE CHARMING,
the latest installment in
THE FORTUNES OF TEXAS:
ALL FORTUNE'S CHILDREN.

Joaquin nodded. "It was interesting. I saw a side of your father I'd never seen before. I have acquired a brand-new appreciation for him."

"That makes me so happy. You don't even know. I wish everyone could see him the way you do."

"Thanks for having him invite me."

Zoe held up her hand. "Actually, all I did was ask him if you were coming tonight, and he's the one who decided to invite you. He really likes you, Joaquin. And so do I."

He was silent for a moment, just looking at her in a way that she couldn't read. For a second, she was afraid he was going to friend-zone her again.

"I like you, too, Zoe. You know what I like most about you?"

She shook her head.

"You always see the best in everyone, even in me. I know I haven't been the easiest person to get to know."

Zoe laughed. Even if he was hard to get to know, Joaquin obviously had no idea what a great guy he was.

"I wish I could claim that as a heroic quality," she said. "But it's not hard to see the good in you. I mean, good grief, half the women in the office are in love with you."

He made a face that said he didn't believe her.

"But I don't want to share you."

He answered her by lowering his head and covering her mouth with his. It was a kiss that she felt all the way down to her curled toes.

When they finally came up for air, he said, "In case you're wondering, I just made a move on you."

Don't miss
FORTUNE'S PRINCE CHARMING
by Nancy Robards Thompson,
available May 2016 wherever
Harlequin® Special Edition books and ebooks are sold.

www.Harlequin.com

Turn your love of reading into rewards you'll love with
Harlequin My Rewards

MYR16R

HARLEQUIN®

A *Romance* FOR EVERY MOOD™

JUST CAN'T GET ENOUGH?

Join our social communities
and talk to us online.

You will have access to the latest
news on upcoming titles and special
promotions, but most importantly,
you can talk to other fans about your
favorite Harlequin reads.

Harlequin.com/Community

Facebook.com/HarlequinBooks

Twitter.com/HarlequinBooks

Pinterest.com/HarlequinBooks

Love the Harlequin book you just read?

Your opinion matters.

Review this book on your favorite book site, review site, blog or your own social media properties and share your opinion with other readers!

THE WORLD IS BETTER
WITH
Romance

Harlequin has everything from contemporary, passionate and heartwarming to suspenseful and inspirational stories.

**Whatever your mood,
we have a romance just for you!**

Connect with us to find your next great read, special offers and more.

f /HarlequinBooks

@HarlequinBooks

www.HarlequinBlog.com

www.Harlequin.com/Newsletters

HARLEQUIN®

A *Romance* FOR EVERY MOOD™

www.Harlequin.com